The Awful Truth

Jessica ran blindly down the hall. At last she got to the girls rest room and rushed inside. To her relief, the rest room was empty. She leaned against a sink, staring into the mirror on the wall. Her eyes blurred with hot tears.

How much longer can I go on pretending? *Jessica wondered. She knew that sooner or later someone was bound to figure out the truth.* Maybe I should just admit it to everyone, *she thought.*

"No!" *Jessica muttered. It was just too humiliating to tell anyone, even her mother. And she could never admit it to Elizabeth.*

No, as long as she could hide the truth, no one would ever know that Jessica had been lying. No one could know that Jessica still hadn't started her period. No one.

Bantam Books in the SWEET VALLEY TWINS series. Ask your bookseller for the books you have missed.

SWEET VALLEY TWINS

Jessica's Secret

Written by
Jamie Suzanne

Created by
FRANCINE PASCAL

BANTAM BOOKS
TORONTO · NEW YORK · LONDON · SYDNEY · AUCKLAND

JESSICA'S SECRET

A BANTAM BOOK 0 553 40186 6

Originally published in U.S.A. by Bantam Skylark Books

First publication in Great Britain

PRINTING HISTORY
Bantam edition published 1990
Reprinted 1991

Sweet Valley High® and Sweet Valley Twins are registered
trademarks of Francine Pascal.

Conceived by Francine Pascal.

Produced by Daniel Weiss Associates, Inc., 27 West 20th
Street,
New York, NY 10011

Cover art by James Mathewuse

Bantam Books are published by Transworld Publishers Ltd.,
61–63 Uxbridge Road, Ealing, London W5 5SA,
in Australia by Transworld Publishers (Australia) Pty. Ltd.,
15–23 Helles Avenue, Moorebank, NSW 2170, and in New
Zealand by Transworld Publishers (N.Z.) Ltd., Cnr. Moselle
and Waipareira Avenues, Henderson, Auckland.

Made and printed in Great Britain by
BPCC Hazell Books
Aylesbury, Bucks, England
Member of BPCC Ltd.

Jessica's Secret

One

"Jessica!" Elizabeth Wakefield called as she burst into her twin sister's room. Elizabeth was grinning broadly. Something very exciting and wonderful had just happened—something only her twin could truly understand.

Jessica was standing in front of her full-length mirror, carefully twisting her hair into a complicated braid. The latest copy of *Image Magazine* lay on her unmade bed. It was opened to an article on new hair styles.

Elizabeth hopped over a mound of clothes on the floor and joined Jessica in front of the mirror.

"What do you think, Lizzie?" Jessica asked, turning her head to give Elizabeth a better view of her braid.

"It looks great, Jess," Elizabeth said. "Although I don't know how you can think about your hair at a time like this. We have much more important things to think about today."

"What's so great about today?" Jessica asked, frowning at her image in the mirror. "Besides the fact that it's Wednesday, which means it's practically Thursday, which means it's almost the weekend?"

Elizabeth smiled. "You, of all people, know what I mean." She examined her own reflection thoughtfully. "Do I look any different to you?" she asked Jessica.

"What do you mean, different?" Jessica asked.

"Different than I did this morning," Elizabeth prompted with a sly grin.

Jessica turned from the mirror and examined her twin closely. "Well," she said at last, "you were wearing different barrettes this morning. Actually, Elizabeth, I liked the other ones better." She turned her attention back to the mirror. "But you know, now that you mention it, I think I look different. More mature."

Elizabeth shook her head.

"I think it's this hair style," Jessica decided.

Elizabeth didn't seem to hear. She twirled lightly across the room and stopped in front of the window. Jessica came and stood beside her.

Anyone looking up at that window would

have seen two girls who were mirror images of each other. Both had long, silky blond hair and sparkling, blue-green eyes framed by long lashes. When they smiled, they had matching dimples in their left cheeks. The twins were tanned a golden brown from spending so much time in the California sunshine and sometimes, even their good friends had trouble telling them apart.

But that was where their similarities ended. Their personalities were as different as their looks were identical. Elizabeth was the more serious, thoughtful twin. She enjoyed working on the sixth-grade newspaper, and she hoped to become a journalist someday. Her idea of a good time was curling up with a mystery novel, or spending time with one of her closest friends.

Jessica, on the other hand, was much more adventurous. She loved gossip, boys, and parties. She belonged to the Unicorns, an exclusive club of girls who considered themselves the prettiest and most popular girls at Sweet Valley Middle School. Elizabeth had nicknamed the Unicorns "the Snob Squad." She didn't understand how Jessica could spend so much time with them. She had a completely different set of friends, most of whom Jessica considered dull and boring.

In spite of their differences, the twins had always been best friends. They'd spent many special moments together and they shared a magical bond that nobody else could understand.

Elizabeth smiled at her twin. "Actually, I do think I look just a little bit more mature," she mused.

"You do?" Jessica asked doubtfully. Everyone knew that Jessica was the more sophisticated, older-looking twin. After all, she always wore the most fashionable clothes, and often wore lip gloss and a touch of mascara.

"Well, maybe not," Elizabeth admitted. "But ever since I got it, I *feel* older."

"It?" Jessica echoed.

"My period, silly!" Elizabeth exclaimed. "Jessica, can you believe it really happened? It still hasn't quite sunk in."

Jessica shook her head slowly.

"This means we're—what was it our fifth-grade gym teacher used to say?" Elizabeth giggled at the memory. " 'Blossoming into womanhood.' "

Elizabeth fell back onto Jessica's bed. "You know," she said, "I wasn't sure how I'd feel. I have a little stomach ache today, but that's about all." She propped herself up on her elbows, smiling at a sudden thought. "I'm glad we were at home when it started, and not stuck at school or something!"

Jessica didn't respond. She dropped down

next to Elizabeth on the bed, and stared off into space.

For the first time Elizabeth noticed that her twin looked a little pale. She realized it was possible Jessica wasn't feeling as well as she was. After all, even though they were twins, they couldn't expect their bodies to behave in precisely the same way!

"Poor Jess," Elizabeth said sympathetically. She sat up and put her arm around Jessica's shoulders. "Are you feeling OK?"

"Well . . ." Jessica began.

"We'll ask Mom," Elizabeth interrupted her. "I'm sure she'll know what to do to make you feel better."

Elizabeth knew that when it came to aches and pains, Jessica had a tendency to be a little dramatic. If Elizabeth was a bit tired, she could always count on Jessica to be completely exhausted.

"Hey!" Elizabeth said suddenly. "You haven't told Mom yet, have you?"

"No," Jessica answered softly.

"Good! Then we can surprise her together!"

"It'll be a surprise, all right," Jessica mumbled.

"Somehow I always thought things would always stay the same." Elizabeth said. "But this is really important. It's even more important than . . ." She paused, trying to think of just the right comparison. But there really *was* no comparison.

"Than going on your first date," Jessica offered.

"Or getting a driver's license!" Elizabeth suggested.

"Or going to the prom," Jessica continued. Her face was very serious.

"Let's go downstairs and tell Mom right now!" Elizabeth urged.

"OK," Jessica muttered.

Elizabeth flew down the stairs, and Jessica trudged slowly behind her. They found Mrs. Wakefield, who worked part-time as an interior designer, sitting on the couch, examining fabric samples she'd brought home from work.

When the girls entered the room, Mrs. Wakefield looked up and smiled. "Hi there," she said. "What's new?"

"Nothing much," Elizabeth said as casually as she could. She looked over at Jessica to see if her twin wanted to make their big announcement. But Jessica, who had plopped into a chair, was silent.

I guess it's up to me, Elizabeth thought.

"We may eat a little late tonight," their mother said. "I've got a big deadline coming up and I want to get some work done before I start dinner."

"That's all right, Mom," Elizabeth said. "We'll give you a hand."

Mrs. Wakefield smiled. "Thanks, girls," she said. She turned her attention back to a pile of fabric swatches.

"Mom," Elizabeth began, trying to contain the big smile she felt breaking out on her face, "we're not exactly your *girls* anymore."

"Why? Did you find another mother you like better?" Mrs. Wakefield teased. She was still studying her samples.

Then suddenly she looked up at Elizabeth. She looked surprised. "You don't mean . . ."

Elizabeth nodded.

"That's wonderful!" Mrs. Wakefield jumped to her feet and ran over and embraced Elizabeth and then Jessica. "Oh, I can't believe it! You're growing up so fast!" she exclaimed.

"It's really not such a big deal, Mom," Jessica said irritably, crossing her arms over her chest.

Mrs. Wakefield gave Jessica an understanding smile and reached for her hand. "Come here," she said. "Let's sit down on the couch together for a minute."

The twins settled on the couch with their

mother between them. She draped an arm around each girl's shoulder.

"Even if you don't think this is such a big deal now, Jessica," Mrs. Wakefield began, "someday you'll realize just how important today is. Do either of you have any questions?"

"You already gave us the facts-of-life talk, Mom," Elizabeth reminded her with a smile. "Right, Jess?"

"Like I said, it's no big deal," Jessica repeated.

"I don't think Jessica feels very well," Elizabeth explained to their mother.

"I'm *fine*," Jessica growled.

"Well, that's perfectly natural," Mrs. Wakefield said. "Why don't I get you the heating pad, Jessica? You can lie here on the couch until dinner's ready."

"Would you guys just leave me *alone*?" Jessica demanded irritably.

"I know what you need, Jessica," Mrs. Wakefield said brightly. "I'm going to fix you two an extra special dinner in honor of this momentous occasion. Anything you want. Your wish is my command!"

"Anything?" Jessica raised an eyebrow.

"Anything," Mrs. Wakefield repeated.

"Spaghetti and meatballs?" Jessica suggested.

"Sure!" her mother agreed. "And what about you, Elizabeth? Anything special you'd like?"

"Hmm." Elizabeth thought for a minute. "Garlic bread?"

"And cream puffs for dessert?" Jessica said.

Mrs. Wakefield laughed. "Well, if I'm going to fix this gourmet feast, I'd better get started," she said.

"What about your design project?" Elizabeth asked.

"Oh, that can wait," Mrs. Wakefield assured her. "After all, how often does a mom get to celebrate such a big occasion?"

"I know," Elizabeth said as she leaped off the couch. "I'll help you in the kitchen. Then you'll have time to get more work done on your project."

"I'll help, too," Jessica volunteered quietly.

"Are you sure you feel like it, honey?" Mrs. Wakefield asked Jessica.

Jessica nodded.

"Great," Elizabeth said. "I'll go get started, then." She disappeared into the kitchen.

Jessica got up from the couch slowly. "Mom?" she asked, in a voice that was just a whisper.

"Yes, hon?"

"How old were you when you first got your period?"

"I was just about your age," Mrs. Wakefield answered. "Maybe a little older. Why?"

"Just curious," Jessica said.

In the kitchen, Mrs. Wakefield started the meatballs, while Elizabeth and Jessica made a salad. Once that was done, all three began working on the cream puffs.

"Will you make these for us *every* month, Mom?" Elizabeth joked.

"I wouldn't count on it," Mrs. Wakefield said with a smile. "You'll be getting your period for the next forty years!"

"Forty *years*?" Jessica echoed in disbelief. "That's practically forever!"

Just then Steven came barrelling through the kitchen door. He was carrying his basketball under one arm.

"How was practice, honey?" Mrs. Wakefield asked.

"The same as always," Steven answered. He walked over to the kitchen counter where Elizabeth and Jessica were mixing the filling for the cream puffs. "What's for dinner?" he asked as he stuck a finger into the bowl.

"Steven!" Jessica cried.

"You might try using a spoon," Mrs. Wakefield said.

"He's too *uncivilized*," Jessica said. "Besides,

Steven, these cream puffs are in honor of Lizzie and me."

"What's the occasion?" Steven demanded, giving Jessica a doubtful look.

Jessica exchanged smiles with Elizabeth. "Nothing *you'd* understand," Jessica told him.

The twins dissolved into giggles, and Steven gave Mrs. Wakefield a helpless shrug.

"Girls!" he groaned.

Right before they went to bed that night, Jessica appeared in Elizabeth's bedroom doorway. Elizabeth was already in bed, reading a mystery by Amanda Howard.

"I've been thinking, Lizzie," Jessica said thoughtfully. She sat down on the end of Elizabeth's bed. "Now that we're officially grown up, don't you think Mom and Dad should treat us like adults?"

Elizabeth could tell Jessica was about to present one of her schemes. "Well," she answered slowly, "that depends. What do you have in mind?"

"Remember when I asked if we could go visit Robin in San Diego, and Mom and Dad said we weren't ready to go on such a long trip alone?"

Robin was one of their favorite cousins. She

was just a few months younger than the twins. Last year Robin's father, who worked for a computer company, had been transferred to France for the entire year. The family had just recently moved back to San Diego, and both Elizabeth and Jessica were anxious to see Robin.

"You think Mom and Dad might let us go see her by ourselves, now that we're more mature?" Elizabeth asked.

"I'm sure of it," Jessica said firmly.

Elizabeth recognized the determined look in her sister's eyes. "I hope you're right," she said. "I'd love to see Robin again and hear all about France."

"Don't worry. We're going to go," Jessica said confidently. "If we're going to *be* adults, then we'd better get treated like adults."

Two

◇

"Did you tell anybody?" Elizabeth asked Jessica as they walked home after school the next day.

Jessica shrugged. "No. Why should I?"

Elizabeth found it hard to believe that Jessica hadn't told *anyone* about getting her period. Not even Lila Fowler, who was her best friend. Next to Elizabeth.

"I told Amy this morning," Elizabeth confided. Amy Sutton was one of her closest friends.

"Can we talk about this another time?" Jessica snapped. "We have much more important things to think about."

"Sure," Elizabeth said uncertainly, realizing they didn't feel the same way about what had happened to them.

"Anyway," Jessica said, abruptly changing

the subject, "let's ask Mom and Dad about San Diego at dinner tonight. I'll start by talking about how much I've missed Robin. Then you jump in, Elizabeth."

"Jump in?"

"Say you're curious about what it's like to live in France, or something," Jessica explained.

"Don't you think we should just come right out and ask them?" Elizabeth suggested.

"No! It's much better to warm them up first. Trust me." Jessica's eyes lit up with inspiration. "Maybe we should make them some great dessert for dinner!"

"If you think Mom and Dad are going to let us go just because we make them dessert, then you don't know them very well," Elizabeth said with a laugh.

"Still, it couldn't hurt," Jessica pointed out.

"Please, whatever you do—no more cream puffs! I thought I was going to explode last night!"

"I promise," Jessica said, smiling.

"It would be terrific to see Robin," Elizabeth said after a pause.

"I bet she owns all the latest Parisian fashions," Jessica said.

"Somehow I can't imagine Robin wearing anything too sophisticated," Elizabeth joked.

"I'll bet she's got all the newest styles," Jessica insisted. "Speaking of styles, I want to ride over to Valley Pharmacy and pick up the newest copy of *Image*. Want to come along?"

"More hair styles?" Elizabeth teased.

"Actually, this month they're doing color combinations," Jessica answered.

"Sure, I'll go with you," Elizabeth said. "We've got to get some, uh, supplies, anyway."

Jessica frowned. "What supplies?" she asked, looking puzzled.

"*You* know."

Suddenly a look of recognition dawned on Jessica's face. "Oh, *those* supplies," she murmured.

"Know what Amy said when I told her about us?" Elizabeth asked.

"That we're entering womanhood?" Jessica suggested.

"Good guess." Elizabeth giggled. "But no. She said she was kind of jealous. She understands that everybody's different and lots of girls don't start until they're older, but still, she felt left out."

"What did you tell her?" Jessica asked as they turned onto their driveway.

"I told her not to worry. It's not as if this is a competition. And I told her that she was lucky, because I'd be the guinea pig and could tell her all about it." Elizabeth paused at the front door.

"I hope that made her feel a little better. Do you think it did?"

"Probably not," Jessica said as she pushed by Elizabeth into the house.

After snacking on some oatmeal cookies and apples, the twins hopped on their bikes and headed for Valley Pharmacy.

When they got to the pharmacy, they quickly locked up their bikes and went in. Elizabeth followed Jessica straight to the magazine section. Jessica began leafing through *SMASH!*, a fan magazine filled with color pictures of rock bands and TV stars.

"Look," she said excitedly, "here's a picture of Johnny Buck when he was only a baby. Wasn't he adorable?"

Elizabeth glanced at the magazine. "Kind of chubby, don't you think?" she asked.

"That's just baby fat!" Jessica exclaimed. Johnny Buck was one of Jessica's favorite rock stars. She had a life-size poster of him on her bedroom wall.

"Are you ready to go?" Elizabeth asked.

"Go?" Jessica said. "We just got here, Lizzie! I haven't even had a chance to check out the makeup section yet!"

Elizabeth tapped her foot impatiently. "It's just that I'm kind of nervous. About buying the stuff, I mean. I want to get it over with."

"All right," Jessica said reluctantly.

"Thanks, Jess," Elizabeth said.

Jessica exchanged *SMASH!* for the newest issue of *Image*. "So where is this stuff, anyway?" she whispered to Elizabeth as she tucked the magazine under her arm.

"Over there, I think." Elizabeth pointed to the corner of the store where a large sign said PERSONAL CARE.

They were halfway down the aisle when Jessica grabbed Elizabeth's arm. "Stop!" she hissed.

"What's wrong?"

"I just want to make sure there isn't anyone here we know." Jessica peeked over the rows of deodorant in front of her. "Nope," she said at last. "The coast is clear."

"Good." Elizabeth sighed. "Let's get this over with!"

They grabbed what they needed and headed to where the cashiers stood. Jessica hesitated. There were two registers. Behind one stood a middle-aged woman wearing round glasses. Stationed behind the other register was an incredibly cute boy who looked about seventeen.

"Get in the left line," Jessica urged Elizabeth.

"But the right one is so much shorter . . . *Oh.*" Elizabeth's gaze landed on the boy. "Good choice, Jess," she agreed. Somehow she did not want to have to be waited on by a boy.

Suddenly Elizabeth clutched at her sister's arm. "Jessica," she whispered hoarsely. "Whatever you do, *don't turn around!*"

Naturally, Jessica immediately spun around. What she saw made her face go white.

Heading straight for their check-out counter was Bruce Patman, one of the cutest boys in the seventh grade, accompanied by some other boys in their class, including Todd Wilkins. Jessica secretly thought Todd was really cute. If Todd saw her now, she was sure she would literally die from humiliation.

Jessica's head snapped back. "We're doomed," she moaned.

"Do you think they saw us?" Elizabeth asked. She felt panicky despite the fact that she didn't even like Bruce Patman.

Jessica held her magazine in front of her face and peeked over the top. Bruce and his friends had decided to get on the other register line. They were studying a comic book that Bruce was holding.

"I don't think they noticed us—yet," Jessica whispered, turning her back to the boys. "Let's make a run for it, Elizabeth! We can dump our stuff on a shelf on the way out and come back later when the coast is clear."

"Are these together?" the cashier asked loudly, snapping them back to reality.

"Yes," Elizabeth mumbled.

In the next line, they could hear Bruce and his friends talking and laughing.

"Hang in there, Jess," Elizabeth whispered in her sister's ear. "We're almost out of here."

The cashier picked up Jessica's magazine and rang up the price. Then she lifted up the box, turning it over and over, looking for the price tag.

"How much are these, do you know?" the cashier demanded.

Elizabeth shook her head apologetically. Her cheeks were pink.

"You know?" the cashier asked Jessica.

Jessica began to blush, too. "No, I don't."

"Hey, Paul," the cashier yelled to the cute boy at the next register. "You know how much these are?" She was waving the box high in the air.

He looked up from his register. "What brand?" he called back. "Young Miss?"

It seemed to the twins that the entire store had grown perfectly silent.

"Two eighty-nine," the boy called back.

"See?" the cashier said happily. "They're on sale. I saved you forty cents."

Neither Elizabeth nor Jessica felt particularly grateful as they left the store. In fact, Jessica was convinced that she'd just lost her chance to go out with Todd someday.

"I am never setting foot in that drug store again!" Jessica vowed when they were safely at home again. "And I am never going to be able to look any of those boys in the face again."

Elizabeth couldn't help but giggle. "Do you think they actually noticed us?"

"How could they have missed us?" Jessica retorted. "I'm sure I heard them laughing as we left the store."

Three

◇

"That was a terrific dinner, Mom," Jessica said enthusiastically. "You're a great cook!"

"Watch out. She wants something," Steven warned.

Jessica gave Steven a frosty look. Dinner was almost over, and she had decided it was time to bring up the subject of a visit to Robin's.

"I'm glad you liked it," Mrs. Wakefield said.

"I *loved* it!" Jessica said, smiling.

"She *definitely* wants something," Steven grumbled.

"By the way," Jessica began, looking thoughtfully at her parents, "you know who I've been thinking about a lot lately?"

"Who?" Mr. Wakefield asked.

"Robin," Jessica answered, a faraway look in

her eyes. "It's been a long time since we've seen her, you know."

Elizabeth suddenly jumped; she felt a sharp kick on her shin. "Ouch!" she said, frowning across the table at Jessica.

Jessica smiled sweetly, the picture of innocence.

"I miss Robin, too," Elizabeth offered, glaring at her sister. "I wonder what it was like living in France," she added.

"Robin could probably teach us a lot about French culture," Jessica said in an earnest voice. "Seeing her again would be very educational."

"Oh, brother!" Steven groaned. "Talk about laying it on thick!"

Mr. and Mrs. Wakefield exchanged smiles.

"I don't know what you're talking about, Steven," Jessica said. "Elizabeth and I just happen to miss our very favorite cousin, that's all. Don't we, Lizzie?"

"Ouch!" Elizabeth groaned as she received her second "hint" of the evening. "Uh, yes."

"I hate to interrupt this fine performance," Mr. Wakefield said, "but maybe I can save all of us some time and keep Elizabeth's shins from turning completely black and blue." He winked at Elizabeth. "The answer to your question is yes."

"Yes?" Jessica echoed. She hadn't even asked yet!

"What question?" Steven demanded.

"I believe your sisters were going to ask us if they could visit their cousin in San Diego," Mr. Wakefield explained with a mischievous grin.

"Oh, Daddy, that's wonderful!" Elizabeth exclaimed.

But Jessica still wasn't convinced. "You mean, alone?" she asked doubtfully. "We get to go to San Diego by ourselves?"

"Isn't that what you wanted?" Mrs. Wakefield asked.

"Yes, but . . ." Jessica trailed off. Somehow, she couldn't quite believe what she was hearing.

"Your father and I know we can trust you to behave like adults," Mrs. Wakefield said.

"Since when?" Steven asked.

"Steven, that's enough," Mr. Wakefield warned.

"What made you change your minds?" Jessica asked.

"You're more mature now," Mr. Wakefield remarked, and he gave the twins a private wink.

Steven groaned.

"Jess, can you believe it?" Elizabeth cried. Then she turned to her mother. "When can we go?"

"Well, next week there's a four-day weekend," Mrs. Wakefield pointed out. "School will be closed for teacher conferences. You could leave on Thursday and come back on Sunday.

"Four whole days?" Jessica cried in surprise. "I can't believe it!"

"I'll call Aunt Nancy this evening to see if it's all right," Mrs. Wakefield added.

"So where do *I* get to go?" Steven demanded. He looked a little put out.

"You get to be an only child for a while," Mrs. Wakefield told him.

"Yeah!" Steven brightened. "No sisters for four days! That sounds great. Do you think the shrimps are mature enough to go someplace for a few years—a foreign country maybe?"

The twins were too excited to pay attention to their brother's teasing. "See? I *told* you I'd convince them!" Jessica whispered to Elizabeth as they began carrying the dirty dishes to the kitchen sink. "Of course, I didn't think it would be quite so easy," she admitted.

"I guess growing up has its advantages," Elizabeth said.

"That's for sure," Jessica agreed. "After we clear the table, let's start planning what to pack, OK?"

"OK!" Elizabeth said.

Upstairs in Jessica's bedroom, the twins began listing everything they wanted to take to Robin's.

"I want to bring my scrapbook," Jessica said, "so Robin can see all the exciting things that have happened to me this year."

"We should take our photo album, too," Elizabeth suggested. "And I want to show her a copy of *The Sweet Valley Sixers.*"

Jessica doubted that Robin would be any more interested in the school newspaper than *she* was. "Do you really think Robin will want to read some boring story about the student council?" Jessica asked.

"Sure," Elizabeth responded. "Robin's always loved hearing about our school."

Jessica twirled a strand of hair around her finger. "Yes, but she's been in France for an entire year. They're very sophisticated there, you know."

"So?"

"So Robin will probably want to hear about more exciting things. Like the Unicorns, for example."

Elizabeth didn't say what she was thinking—that the Unicorns were the silliest, snobbiest girls in school. Elizabeth thought it was boring to hear them talk about cute boys, cute clothes, and cute soap opera stars. She was sure Robin would agree with her. Still, she didn't want to argue over Robin with Jessica. Ever since they were little kids, the three of them had been great friends, and Elizabeth didn't want anything to spoil that.

"Remember how Uncle Kirk nicknamed us 'the Three Musketeers' when we were little?" Elizabeth said, trying to change the subject. "We were always getting ourselves into *some* kind of trouble!"

Jessica grinned. "Like that time we spent all afternoon making prank phone calls? How old were we then?"

"Let's see." Elizabeth looked thoughtful. "Third grade, I think."

"Can you believe we ever thought that was funny?" Jessica asked.

"Funny?" Elizabeth said with a smile. "We thought it was *hilarious*!"

Both girls broke into laughter.

Just then they heard Mrs. Wakefield calling them from downstairs.

The twins ran out into the hallway. "Yes, Mom?" Elizabeth called back.

Mrs. Wakefield was standing at the foot of the stairs. "Aunt Nancy is on the phone. She says next week would be a perfect time for you to visit, since Robin will be off from school, too."

"All right!" Jessica cried.

"Pick up the phone and say hello to Robin," Mrs. Wakefield told them.

"Thanks, Mom!" Elizabeth replied.

"Keep it short." Mrs. Wakefield said. "You'll be seeing Robin in a few days and will have plenty of time to catch up then."

Jessica rushed to the hallway telephone and picked up the receiver. "Robin?" she said. "Are you there?"

From her sister's squeal of delight, Elizabeth could tell Robin was on the line. For the next few minutes, Elizabeth listened patiently while Jessica and Robin talked about all the fun the three of them were going to have in San Diego. Finally, Jessica reluctantly handed the phone over to Elizabeth.

"Robin?" Elizabeth said.

"Hi, Lizzie!" Robin answered. "I can't believe you and Jess are really coming to visit! We're going to have a blast!"

"I can't wait!" Elizabeth answered.

"I've got a whole new group of friends I hang out with, and I'm dying for you to meet them. You're going to be so impressed!"

"Girls! Time's up." Mrs. Wakefield called from downstairs.

"But Mom," Jessica yelled, "Elizabeth's barely had a chance to talk to Robin."

"This is long distance," Mrs. Wakefield said sternly.

"Listen, Robin, I've got to go," Elizabeth told her cousin. "But we'll see you next Thursday."

"Great!" Robin exclaimed.

"Bye," Elizabeth said, hanging up the phone.

"Sorry, Elizabeth," Jessica said immediately. "I was so excited, I forgot about the time."

"That's OK," Elizabeth said, as they headed back to Jessica's bedroom. "So, tell me what Robin told you."

"Well, Robin has tons of news," Jessica said as she settled on her bed. "Didn't you think she sounded different?"

"Different? How?" Elizabeth asked. Robin had sounded the same to her, but then, she had only spoken to her for a few seconds.

"It's hard to explain, but she sounded more grown up," Jessica reflected. "She said she has a whole new group of cool friends."

"She told me that, too," Elizabeth said. "You know, I hope she hasn't changed *too* much. I liked her the way she was."

"Don't worry, Elizabeth," Jessica told her cheerfully. "After all, *we've* changed, too. The last time Robin saw us we were sharing the same bedroom and dressing alike. And now look at us! You have the *Sixers* and I have the Unicorns, and we act a lot differently than we did."

Elizabeth smiled. "You're right. We *have* changed." Suddenly an idea hit her. "Jess, do you think Robin's gotten her period yet?"

Jessica's expression darkened. "I doubt it, Elizabeth," she said with a shrug. "Robin *is* a few months younger than we are. And besides, it's really none of our business."

"But—" Elizabeth began.

"You're not going to tell her about us starting, are you?" Jessica interrupted her.

"I hadn't really thought about it. Why?"

Jessica sighed. "Because if she hasn't started yet, there's no reason to make her feel bad."

"Why would she feel bad?" Elizabeth asked.

"And if she *has* already started," Jessica continued, ignoring her sister's question, "then she probably has a few million more interesting things to talk about."

"All right, Jess," Elizabeth said flatly. She didn't think there was any point in arguing about it.

"Good. I'm glad you agree," Jessica responded. "If we're going to be treated like grown-ups, we'd better start acting that way."

*   *   *

Jessica was standing in front of her locker on Friday morning when she spotted Lila Fowler coming down the hallway.

"Lila!" Jessica called. "Come here a minute." She couldn't wait to tell someone about her big trip. "Guess who's going to be in San Diego next week, while all her friends are stuck in boring old Sweet Valley?"

"San Diego!" Lila exclaimed. "You get to go to San Diego?" Her eyes narrowed. "You mean like a family trip, right?"

"Oh, please." Jessica groaned. "Elizabeth and I are going by ourselves." She began dialing her combination lock, waiting to see what Lila's response would be.

"By yourselves?" Lila repeated. She sounded suspicious.

"We're going to visit our cousin Robin," Jessica said importantly. She opened her locker. "She just moved back from living overseas for a year." Jessica paused for effect. "In *Paris*."

Lila's jaw dropped open. "Paris?"

Jessica sorted through the mess at the bottom of her locker. "Robin's very popular," she said over her shoulder. "She's going to take us around to meet all her friends while we're there." Jessica closed her locker and faced Lila. Just as she'd hoped, Lila was green with envy. "Jessica Wake-field," she said glumly, "you are *so* lucky."

"Lucky? How come?" Mary Wallace asked as she joined them.

"She's going to San Diego," Lila explained.

"So?" Mary asked. "I've been there lots of times."

"*Alone*," Lila added meaningfully.

"No parents?" Mary exclaimed. "Way to go, Jess! Not even a chaperone?"

"Well," Jessica said with a sly smile, "just Elizabeth!"

Jessica, Lila, and Mary were discussing how many suitcases Jessica should take on the trip, when they noticed Elizabeth hurrying down the hall toward them.

"Jessica!" Elizabeth said breathlessly as she joined the girls in front of Jessica's locker. "I need to ask you something."

"Can't it wait?" Jessica asked impatiently.

"Well, not exactly," Elizabeth said, casting a pleading look at her sister.

"If I'm late for history again, I'll definitely get a detention," Mary said.

"Mary's right," Lila agreed. "The bell's going to ring any second. I'll help you plan what to pack at lunch, Jess."

"What's the problem?" Jessica asked her sister after her friends had gone.

"I forgot to bring my supplies with me to school today," Elizabeth said in a hushed voice.

"Here." Jessica handed Elizabeth her notebook. "I hardly ever take notes in social studies, anyway."

"No," Elizabeth said with a smile. "I mean, you know, *supplies*. Do you have any I could borrow?"

"No," Jessica said softly. Her face was pale. "I mean . . . I don't have enough for both of us. You'll just have to . . . to ask somebody else!" With that, Jessica spun on her heels and rushed down the hallway. "Jessica?" Elizabeth called as she watched her twin disappear around a corner.

Jessica didn't answer. She ran blindly down the hall, which was now empty. The class bell rang loudly, but she barely even heard it. At last she got to the girls' rest room and rushed inside.

To her relief, the rest room was empty. She dropped her books on the floor and leaned against a sink, staring into the mirror on the wall. Her eyes blurred with hot tears. "What is *wrong* with you?" she demanded of her reflection. Tears rolled down her cheeks.

How much longer can I go on pretending? Jessica wondered. She knew that sooner or later someone was bound to figure out the awful truth. *Maybe I should just admit it to everyone,* she thought.

"No!" Jessica muttered. It was just too humiliating. She couldn't tell anyone, not even her mother. And she could never admit it to Elizabeth.

No, as long as she could hide the truth, no one would ever know that Jessica had been lying. No one could know that Jessica still hadn't started her period. *No one.*

Four

◇

"I was kind of worried about you this morning, Jess," Elizabeth said as she and Jessica were walking home that afternoon.

"How come?" Jessica asked casually.

"You seemed like you were upset about something," Elizabeth replied.

"Me?" Jessica laughed loudly. "I was just late for class. You're such a worrier, Elizabeth!"

Elizabeth smiled with relief. Jessica seemed to be in a much better mood now.

"Let's go to the mall tomorrow," Jessica suggested as they neared home. "We can get new outfits to wear to Robin's."

"Great idea!" Elizabeth agreed. "I've got some money saved up from my allowance and babysitting."

Jessica's face fell. "Oh, I forgot about *money*."

"I thought you'd been saving up," Elizabeth said.

"I was. But then that double album of Melody Power's came out . . ." Jessica's voice trailed off.

"I'll tell you what," Elizabeth said as they turned onto their street. "You can borrow some money from me."

"Lizzie, you're the greatest!" Jessica cried happily. "And I promise I'll pay you right back."

"I know you will," Elizabeth answered. "Besides, I know where to find you if you don't!"

Elizabeth pushed back the curtain of the dressing room at Valley Fashions. "Jessica!" she called. "Let's see!"

Jessica stepped out of the dressing room and into the narrow carpeted area where Elizabeth was waiting.

"What do you think?" she inquired, twirling around so Elizabeth could get the full effect of her outfit. She was wearing an oversize purple top with a purple miniskirt.

"It's great," Elizabeth said. "You look like you just walked out of *Image Magazine*."

Jessica strode past the other dressing rooms like a fashion model on a runway. Then she spun around and walked back to Elizabeth. Elizabeth giggled at her sister and Jessica grinned broadly.

"I like the blouse you have on, Elizabeth," Jessica said.

"Do you really?" Elizabeth asked. "We've been shopping all day and I still can't decide what to get."

Jessica followed Elizabeth back to her dressing room, where Elizabeth examined her blouse in front of the three-way mirror. It was deep turquoise, with puffy sleeves and a round collar. There were little pearl buttons down the front. It wasn't something Jessica would wear, but she thought it looked nice on Elizabeth.

"I think that blouse is really cute," Jessica told her sister. "It brings out the blue in your eyes."

"I think I'll take it, then," Elizabeth said. "How much is the outfit you're wearing?"

"That's the amazing thing," Jessica said brightly. "It's half price. Can you believe it, Lizzie?"

Elizabeth reached for the tag fluttering off Jessica's sleeve. When she read it, she gasped. "Jessica," she said slowly, "if we pool all our money, we can just barely pay for your outfit and my blouse. But we'd have almost nothing left for San Diego!"

Jessica slumped against the wall, looking

dejected. "OK, Elizabeth. You go ahead and buy your blouse," she said. "I'll just wear the same hideous old outfits I always wear."

Elizabeth frowned. She couldn't bear to see Jessica in another bad mood. And this *was* a special occasion. "All right," she said at last. "Let's do it!"

"That's the spirit, Lizzie!" Jessica said. "And when we're broke, at least we'll look good, right?"

"You better believe it!" Elizabeth agreed.

Jessica smiled. Today her secret didn't seem nearly so important. In fact, it felt like nothing had changed at all.

On Monday, Elizabeth and Jessica wore their new clothes to school. At the Unicorner, the Unicorns' special table in the lunchroom, everyone commented on Jessica's purple outfit. Purple was the official color of the Unicorns, and all the members tried to wear something purple every day.

"Did they have any left?" Ellen Riteman asked Jessica. "I'd love to get that outfit."

"I think this was the very last one in the store," Jessica said. She wasn't positive that was true, but she didn't want Ellen to get the exact same outfit she already had.

Jessica picked up her tuna salad sandwich,

and then put it down. She decided to go straight for her apple pie instead. "I'm going to wear this outfit in San Diego," she announced.

"You're so lucky, Jessica," Janet Howell said as she reached into her lunch bag. Janet was an eighth-grader and the president of the Unicorn Club. "We've got four whole days off, and you're the only Unicorn who's doing anything exciting."

Jessica smiled. She loved being the center of attention.

"Does anyone want my potato chips?" Janet asked. She made a face at the little bag of chips and tossed it into the center of the table. "They always make me break out, especially right before my period."

"Me, too," Tamara Chase chimed in. "I can always tell what time of month it is, because I get a pimple right here." She pointed to a spot on her chin.

"The monthly zit fit!" Mary Wallace laughed.

"Gross, you guys!" Lila said. "Some of us are trying to eat here, if you don't mind."

"Really," Jessica muttered in agreement. One minute they were talking about her trip to San Diego, and the next minute they were chattering away about pimples and periods. *What was wrong with everybody lately?* she wondered angrily. No matter where she went, people kept bringing up that same annoying subject. It was almost enough to make you wish you were a boy!

"Here, Jessica." Janet shoved the chips in Jessica's direction. "Why don't you eat these?"

"Why me? What's that supposed to mean?" Jessica demanded.

Janet gave Jessica a surprised look. "I just noticed that you hadn't eaten much of your sandwich," she explained. "I thought maybe you were still hungry. You don't *have* to eat them."

"Oh," Jessica said in a sheepish tone. "Thanks, Janet."

When she thought about it some more, Jessica realized that there was no reason to think any of the Unicorns suspected her secret. She knew that some of the seventh- and eighth-grade Unicorns had already gotten their periods, but that was only natural—after all, they were older. And as for Ellen and Lila, as far as Jessica knew, they were just like she was.

Of course, that was what she used to think about Elizabeth.

Suddenly it occurred to her that Ellen and Lila might have started their periods a long time ago. Maybe they had a secret pact not to tell Jessica the truth. For months they might have been pitying her behind her back. . . .

Lila reached for the potato chips and opened

the package. "Isn't that Elizabeth?" she asked Jessica.

"Where?" Jessica said.

"Talking to Julie Porter, over by the lunch line." Lila crunched on a potato chip. "What is Elizabeth wearing, anyway?" she said. "That blouse looks like something I'd have worn in the fourth grade!"

Some of the other Unicorns twisted around in their seats to see what Lila was talking about.

"You're right, Lila," Ellen agreed eagerly. "She looks like a baby!"

Jessica studied her twin carefully. Elizabeth was wearing her new turquoise blouse and a pair of jeans. Jessica had to admit the blouse *did* look a little old-fashioned, especially compared to her own new outfit. It had looked OK in the mall, but now Jessica realized that for someone who was supposed to be so "mature," Elizabeth didn't dress like it.

"I've always thought it would be fun to have a twin so I could borrow all her clothes," Tamara mused. "Too bad for Jessica that her twin has no taste!"

Jessica started to defend Elizabeth. After all, she *had* told her sister to go ahead and buy the blouse. But something stopped her. *Elizabeth is grown up enough to defend herself*, Jessica thought irritably. *It's not my fault if she doesn't have a flair for fashion.*

Just then Jessica looked up and saw Elizabeth approaching the Unicorner. Out of the corner of her eye, Jessica caught a glimpse of Lila smirking. "Did I say fourth grade?" Lila whispered to Ellen. "That blouse reminds me more of kindergarten!"

Jessica gritted her teeth. Lately it seemed like Elizabeth was going out of her way to embarrass her.

"Hi, Jess," Elizabeth said as she neared Jessica's chair. "I just wanted to remind you that Mom's taking us shopping right after school to get a birthday present for Stacey." Stacey, Robin's little sister, was going to turn eight while the twins were visiting.

"Why don't you go without me?" Jessica said tensely. "I've got a Boosters practice after school, anyway." The Boosters were a cheering and baton squad that Jessica belonged to.

"But—" Elizabeth began.

"Besides," Jessica interrupted, "you're already dressed like an eight-year-old, Elizabeth. You ought to be able to pick Stacey's present with no problem."

Lila covered her mouth to hide a smile. Some of the other Unicorns stared in surprise at Jessica's outburst.

But no one was more surprised than Elizabeth. Her mouth dropped open and her cheeks grew bright red. For a long moment she stood silent, waiting for Jessica to explain herself.

At last Elizabeth turned and rushed away without saying another word.

"What a baby," Jessica mumbled under her breath as she watched her sister run off.

Elizabeth didn't see Jessica again until history class that afternoon. Mr. Nydick, their teacher, had asked the class to meet in the school library so they could do research for the new project he'd assigned. The week before he'd had each student draw the name of a U.S. president out of a bag. After reading about the president's accomplishments, they would give an oral report on their findings.

"Who'd you get for the pick-a-prez project?" Amy asked Elizabeth as they entered the library. Most of their classmates were already scattered around the large room, copying information out of encyclopedias.

"Abraham Lincoln," Elizabeth answered. She stopped at an empty table in the corner of the library and set down her notebook.

"I got John F. Kennedy," Amy said. "Caroline Pearce told me Jessica got stuck with Millard Fillmore! Poor Jessica! She was trying to trade with everybody, but Mr. Nydick told her that was against the rules."

Elizabeth nodded. "Poor Jess."

"Is something wrong?" Amy asked. "Ever since lunch you've seemed kind of quiet."

The two girls took their seats at the table. "Do you like this blouse, Amy?" Elizabeth asked softly.

"A-hem." The girls looked up and saw Ms. Luster, the librarian, passing by. She gave them her famous I'll-only-warn-you-once look and moved on.

"I already told you I like it," Amy whispered. "Why?"

Elizabeth shook her head. "I don't know. Jessica said she thought it was babyish. She was really rude to me when I saw her at lunch."

"Well, you know Jessica," Amy said with a shrug. "She's not exactly Miss Tactful."

Elizabeth scanned the library. Jessica was sitting at a table by herself, thumbing through a thick book.

"Besides," Amy continued, "you two just have different tastes. Personally, I prefer your clothes, Elizabeth. Would you rather dress like a regular human being, or look like the star of a music video?"

Elizabeth tried to smile. It wasn't just the blouse she cared about, it was the way Jessica had been treating her lately. One minute she was fine, and the next minute she acted like she was furious over something.

For a moment Elizabeth considered going over to her sister and trying to straighten things out. But she just couldn't bring herself to do it. Jessica had hurt *her* feelings, after all. It was Jessica who should apologize.

Jessica looked up from her book and groaned loudly. Even Mr. Nydick, who was a little hard of hearing, heard her from halfway across the library. He frowned and put his finger to his lips.

Jessica had spent an entire half-hour reading a biography of President Fillmore. As far as she could tell, the only interesting thing about the man was the fact that his mother had the nerve to name him Millard.

The way her luck had been running lately, it figured she'd get stuck with such a boring president. Elizabeth, of course, had picked Abraham Lincoln. *Talk about an easy report!* Jessica said to herself.

Jessica thought back to the conversation at the Unicorner earlier. What if she really was the only one who hadn't gotten her period yet? And what if she *never* got it?

Jessica chewed anxiously on the end of her pen, trying to stop worrying. But no matter how hard she tried to concentrate on Millard Fillmore, all her resentment kept bubbling up. It just wasn't fair that Elizabeth had started without her. Nothing seemed fair anymore.

Five

◇

Elizabeth slid open the glass doors that led to the patio in the Wakefields' backyard. It was Wednesday—two days after Jessica's outburst at lunch—and things between her and Jessica hadn't improved much since then. Elizabeth wanted to be alone for a while to think things over, and she knew just where to go—to her thinking seat, which was a wide, low branch of a pine tree in the Wakefields' backyard. It was where the twins had always gone to work out their problems when they were younger. But Jessica no longer went there, claiming it was for babies and that she'd outgrown it.

"Hi, Lizzie," her mother called as Elizabeth headed toward the tree. Mrs. Wakefield was kneeling in her flower garden. She was wearing an old shirt and a torn pair of jeans. "Have you and Jessica started packing yet?" she asked.

"No," Elizabeth answered quietly.

"Well, be sure you get it done this evening," Mrs. Wakefield said. She pulled a weed out of the ground. "Your bus leaves early tomorrow."

"Jessica's still at her Unicorn meeting," Elizabeth said. "We'll pack after dinner."

"Good." Mrs. Wakefield wiped her brow with the back of her arm. "Are you excited?"

"Sure," Elizabeth said, trying to sound enthusiastic. "I can't wait to see Robin." She nodded toward the big tree. "I'm going down to the thinking seat, Mom. Call me when it's time to set the table for dinner, OK?"

"Sure, hon."

Usually just coming to the thinking seat made Elizabeth feel better, but instead she felt confused and anxious. She should have been feeling wonderful, too. She had four days off from school, and she was about to go visit her very favorite cousin with Jessica.

Unfortunately, Jessica was the problem. She *still* hadn't apologized. In fact, she'd acted as if nothing unusual had happened between them.

"Is there room for two?"

Elizabeth twisted around to find her mother

heading toward the thinking seat. "Of course," she said, smiling.

Mrs. Wakefield joined Elizabeth. "I can see why you like it here," she said. "It's very peaceful."

"Coming here helps me think," Elizabeth told her.

"I remember you and Jessica used to play here together for hours and hours," Mrs. Wakefield recalled.

"That was ages ago," Elizabeth said sadly. "Jessica never comes here anymore."

Mrs. Wakefield nodded. "Lots of things have changed, haven't they, honey?"

"Mom," Elizabeth cried, "*everything's* changed. I feel like I can't even talk to Jessica anymore! And the other day . . ." Elizabeth trailed off.

"What about the other day?" Mrs. Wakefield prompted.

"Well, I was wearing my new blouse. The one I got at the mall last weekend—"

"You look pretty in that blouse," her mother interrupted.

"Jessica didn't think so," Elizabeth told her.

"What do you mean?" Mrs. Wakefield asked.

"She made fun of me for wearing it at lunch on Monday. In front of all the Unicorns," Elizabeth said quietly. "And she hasn't apologized."

"I'm sure she didn't mean to hurt your feelings," Mrs. Wakefield said.

"I don't think she *cares* whether or not she hurt my feelings," Elizabeth exclaimed. "I think she's angry with me, but I can't figure out why."

Mrs. Wakefield gave Elizabeth a smile. "You know," she said, "you and Jessica are going through a very emotional time in your lives. You're growing up, and changing very quickly. Try to understand, that's why your sister may not always be easy to get along with. If you're patient, I promise this will pass before you know it."

"I'm not so sure," Elizabeth said doubtfully.

"Trust me. When I was your age I felt like I was on a roller coaster. One day I'd be happy, the next day I'd be sad. It takes your body a while to get used to all these changes." She squeezed Elizabeth's hand. "You'll see. You and Jessica will be as close as ever soon. Maybe this trip to Robin's will help."

"I hope so," Elizabeth responded. It seemed like she had already been waiting for an eternity.

When Elizabeth went back into the house, Jessica was home from her Unicorn meeting. She was upstairs in her bedroom, carefully packing her suitcase. "Lizzie, you'll be so impressed with my organization," Jessica said proudly.

Elizabeth stared at the suitcase on Jessica's bed. It was stuffed with dozens of outfits. It looked like Jessica had packed every piece of clothing she owned!

Elizabeth peeked into her sister's closet. It was nearly empty.

"Jessica!" she exclaimed. "What did you do? Pack your entire wardrobe?"

"Just the essentials," Jessica said lightly.

"How are you going to close the suitcase?" Elizabeth asked.

"Very carefully!" Jessica joked.

Elizabeth giggled. "And exactly how many pairs of socks are you bringing?"

"Just a few," Jessica answered evasively.

Elizabeth counted. "You call thirteen pairs of socks 'a few'?" she asked. "We're going for four days, not four months!"

Jessica opened her mouth to protest. But when she met Elizabeth's eyes, she couldn't help but laugh. "OK," she admitted, "maybe I did get a little carried away with the socks. But no matter what you say, I'm absolutely, positively bringing my life-size poster of Johnny Buck!"

Elizabeth's jaw dropped in amazement. "Jessica, you have *got* to be kidding me!"

Jessica's eyes sparkled with amusement. "Actually, Lizzie, you're right. I was kidding. Please, give me *some* credit!"

Elizabeth laughed with relief. This was a lot more like the old Jessica she'd been missing.

Jessica removed two pairs of socks from the top of her suitcase. "There," she said with a satisfied smile. "I'm finished."

Mrs. Wakefield and Steven drove the twins to the bus station on Thursday.

As soon as they arrived at the station, Steven jumped out of the Wakefields' maroon van and began unloading the twins' suitcases.

"What did you pack in here, anyway?" Steven grunted as he removed Jessica's suitcase from the back of the van. "Bowling balls?"

"I think Jessica packed everything but the kitchen sink," Mrs. Wakefield teased.

"Trust me," Steven complained, "she packed that, too!"

"Well, if you're going to be such a baby, *I'll* carry it," Jessica said indignantly.

"I don't mind, Jessica," Steven told her. He grinned broadly. "After all, how often do I get to send my sisters away for four whole days?"

"That's enough, Steven," Mrs. Wakefield said.

"You're just jealous," Jessica told him, sharing an excited smile with Elizabeth.

After Mrs. Wakefield purchased the tickets and the twins checked their bags, they all waited for the announcement over the loudspeaker. Finally it came: "Express to San Diego, now departing gate four."

"That's us, Jessica!" Elizabeth cried.

After hugging Mrs. Wakefield and Steven, the twins got into line to board their bus. "I want you two to keep an eye on each other, and be sure to call as soon as you get there," Mrs. Wakefield told them.

"Hey, Mom, did you tell the twins that those tickets are one-way?" Steven said, loud enough for Jessica and Elizabeth to hear.

The girls just laughed and climbed up the steps onto the bus. Through the window they could see Mrs. Wakefield and Steven waiting outside. Both girls waved as the bus slowly pulled out of the lot.

"I am so excited I can hardly stand it," Jessica said. "Doesn't it feel wonderful to be on our own?"

"Well, it's only been about two minutes," Elizabeth pointed out. "But so far I think it's great."

"What do you think we'll do at Robin's?" Jessica wondered.

"Make prank phone calls?" Elizabeth joked. "Last time we visited with Mom, Dad, and Steven, we all went to the San Diego Zoo. That was great!"

Jessica flipped her hair over her shoulder. "It was OK, I suppose. If you're into animals."

"I thought you loved that zoo!" Elizabeth exclaimed.

"I did—then," Jessica replied. "But we're more mature now, Elizabeth. I'm hoping Robin will introduce us to all of her new friends. Maybe she'll even have a party in our honor! I could wear my new purple outfit."

Elizabeth leaned back in her seat and didn't say anything. The mention of Jessica's outfit reminded Elizabeth of her twin's remark earlier that week. Elizabeth still hadn't received an apology, but she'd decided to forgive Jessica anyway. Since yesterday, they'd been getting along much better. And it seemed wrong to ruin the trip over one remark—especially if Mrs. Wakefield was right about Jessica going through a tough time.

But Jessica's remark about the zoo made Elizabeth a little anxious. Personally, she'd *wanted* to go to the zoo, and ride bikes, and tell ghost stories until late in the night. Those were the kinds of things they had always done with Robin. But Jessica seemed to have other ideas.

"Lizzie! Wake up! We're here!"

Elizabeth opened her eyes. She leaned toward the window and saw large buildings and a sign for the bus terminal.

"You slept the whole way," Jessica informed her. "I had to spend most of the trip playing peek-a-boo with the baby in the seat in front of us."

"Sorry." Elizabeth yawned. "I dreamed we were going to the zoo."

Jessica crinkled her nose in distaste. "How boring."

The driver slowed the bus as the station came into view.

Jessica pressed close to the window. "I don't see them anywhere. . . . No, wait! There's Aunt Nancy!" she cried.

"She looks exactly the same," Elizabeth said. "But who's that with her?" A tall, attractive young woman was standing next to their aunt. "And where's Robin?"

"Lizzie!" Jessica exclaimed. "That *is* Robin!"

Six

◇

Elizabeth stared in amazement. Sure enough, the girl was Robin, although she looked nothing like Elizabeth remembered. The last time she had seen Robin, her blond hair was as long as her own. Now it was cut in a sleek chin-length style. She was at least two inches taller, too. In fact, if Elizabeth hadn't known better, she would have sworn that Robin was much older than she was.

"What a great outfit!" Jessica commented. Robin was wearing a black turtleneck, a black skirt, and lots of silver jewelry. She had several strands of silver chains around her neck, thin silver bracelets on her wrists, and big silver hoop earrings. She had on black shoes, and even the sunglasses she was wearing were black.

"Don't you think she looks sort of . . . depressing?" Elizabeth asked.

"Are you kidding? She looks incredibly sophisticated." Jessica gave her sister a knowing look. "Black is very *in*, Elizabeth."

Elizabeth looked again. "I guess you're right," she agreed at last. *Just because Robin looks a little different doesn't mean she's changed*, Elizabeth reminded herself. After all, Jessica went through a new fashion phase every other week!

Together the girls made their way toward the front of the bus. Jessica was the first to jump down. "Robin!" she screamed, rushing toward her cousin.

"Jess!" Robin screamed back, giving Jessica a hug.

Elizabeth ran to join them.

"Elizabeth!" Robin cried, releasing Jessica so she could embrace her.

The twins' uncle and aunt greeted them next. Unlike Robin, they hadn't changed a bit. Uncle Kirk had a red mustache and curly red hair. He was very tall. He'd been a basketball player in college.

Aunt Nancy looked a lot like Mrs. Wakefield. She had blond hair and blue eyes just like the twins' mother.

"It's so wonderful to see you!" Aunt Nancy cried. "You both look so grown up!"

"They look the same to me," Stacey, Robin's little sister, piped up. She had the same bright red hair and freckles as her father.

"Quiet, runt," Robin said.

"Well, you look *much* older, Stacey," Elizabeth told her. "If I didn't know better, I would swear you were eight years old!"

"I *am* eight," Stacey said proudly. "Well, almost. My birthday's tomorrow!"

"No kidding!" Elizabeth pretended to be surprised. "I guess it's lucky we brought that birthday present along, huh, Jessica?"

"Where?" Stacey demanded. "Can I open it now? *Please?*"

"Cool it, shrimp," Robin warned. "It's not even your birthday yet." She rolled her eyes. "Be glad you don't have a younger sister," she told the twins. "She'd drive you totally insane!"

"Try having an older brother!" Jessica moaned. "I'd trade you in a flash."

While their uncle retrieved their bags and loaded them into the family's car, the twins and their cousins piled into the back seat.

"Robin, I can't believe how much older you look!" Jessica marveled. "We hardly recognized you when we drove up. And I *love* what you're wearing!"

"She looks like she's going to a funeral," Stacey declared.

"That's enough, Stace," Aunt Nancy reprimanded.

"If you don't watch out, we'll pull the same trick on you that we pulled on Steven," Robin warned her sister. She looked at Elizabeth and Jessica and all three broke into laughter.

"And what exactly was that, may I ask?" said Uncle Kirk as he settled into the driver's seat. "With the three of you together, I can just imagine!"

The only answer he received was a chorus of giggles.

"Who, us?" Robin asked innocently.

"What did you do to Steven?" Stacey asked. "Was it horrible?"

"Well," Robin said casually, "there was the time we put hot sauce on his hamburger when he wasn't looking."

"Gross!" Stacey groaned.

"He thought it was ketchup," Jessica added.

"Or the time we let the air out of his bike tires," Elizabeth offered.

"Girls!" Aunt Nancy laughed. "You're terrible!"

"Or the time we sprinkled sand into his sleeping bag before we all went on a camp-out," Jessica continued.

"Or—" Robin began.

"I think I've heard more than enough," Uncle Kirk interrupted, chuckling under his breath. "The Three Musketeers strike again!"

Just like old times, Elizabeth thought happily.

Before they knew it, they were pulling into the driveway of Robin's new house. It was in the same neighborhood they'd lived in before they'd gone to France. It was smaller than their old house, and it was more cozy.

Robin led the twins straight to her bedroom. It was decorated in bright colors, and even messier than Jessica's. Big posters of rock groups covered the walls. Two cots had been set up for the twins to sleep on.

"I would have cleaned up more, but I figured you two would understand," Robin said breezily. She sat down on her bed and signaled for the twins to join her. Elizabeth settled on the edge of Robin's bed, but Jessica wandered around the room, inspecting everything.

"Don't you love this poster of Johnny Buck?" Jessica said as she examined Robin's walls. "I have the same exact one at home."

Robin shrugged. "It's OK, I guess. I'm not really into Johnny Buck anymore."

Jessica frowned uncomfortably. "Oh, me either," she said quickly.

Elizabeth gave her sister a surprised look. If Jessica didn't like Johnny Buck anymore, it certainly was news to Elizabeth. Up until about two seconds before, he had been Jessica's very favorite singer.

Suddenly she remembered their promise to their mother. "Hey, Jessica," Elizabeth said, "we really should call home and tell Mom we got here OK."

"Oh, it can wait," Robin said with a wave of her hand. Her silver bracelets jangled whenever she moved. "I've got so much to tell you!"

Jessica and Elizabeth exchanged uneasy glances. "I suppose we could call a little later," Jessica suggested. "I'm sure Mom figures we made it."

Elizabeth wanted to stay and talk as much as Jessica did. But she knew Mrs. Wakefield would be worried if she didn't hear from them. "I'll go call Mom if you want," she offered.

"Thanks, Lizzie," Jessica said. She reached for Robin's school yearbook, which was on the dresser, and began looking through it. "We'll fill you in when you get back."

"Tell Aunt Alice I said hi," Robin added. "And ask her if you can stay longer!"

Elizabeth headed into the hallway. She found her aunt and uncle having cookies in the kitchen with Stacey.

"Would you and Jessica like some lunch?" Aunt Nancy asked.

"Thanks, Aunt Nancy. We ate before we left."

"How about one of your uncle's famous butterscotch cookies, then?" Uncle Kirk slid the plate of cookies toward Elizabeth. "Made especially in your honor, I might add."

"Oh, I love those cookies!" Elizabeth exclaimed. "You make them every time we come to visit." She reached for a cookie and took a big bite. "I need to call my mom, if that's OK," Elizabeth said. "To tell her we made it safely."

"Sure, hon. You can use the phone in the family room," Aunt Nancy said. "Where are Jessica and Robin?"

"Talking," Elizabeth said.

"I'll bet the three of you have a lot of catching up to do." Aunt Nancy smiled. "Send your mom my love."

"I will." Elizabeth took another cookie and headed toward the family room.

"Lizzie?" Stacey called, following after her.

"Yes?" Elizabeth said.

"If you want, you can sleep in my room while you're here. I've got bunk beds, and you can even have the top one." Stacey pushed back a stray lock of her carrot-colored hair. She looked at Elizabeth with eager green eyes.

"Wow, Stace, that's an awfully nice offer," Elizabeth said. She gave Stacey an affectionate pat on the back.

"Honey," Aunt Nancy called from the kitchen, "I think Elizabeth probably wants to sleep with the other girls."

Stacey's face fell. "Robin snores," she warned Elizabeth.

"Tell you what. If her snoring bothers me too much, I'll come sleep in your room," Elizabeth said, smiling. "Deal?"

"Deal!" Stacey exclaimed.

When Elizabeth returned to Robin's bedroom, she found Robin and Jessica sitting together on the bed, giggling over a picture in Robin's yearbook.

"He's adorable!" Jessica cried. "Lizzie, come check out this picture!"

Elizabeth joined them on the bed. She followed Jessica's finger to a photo of a boy who looked about sixteen or seventeen. He had wavy brown hair and a wide smile.

"John W. Anderson," Elizabeth said, reading

the caption beneath the picture. "Varsity football, varsity swim team, and varsity baseball." She glanced up at Robin. "He must be very athletic."

"Don't you think he's cute?" Jessica sighed. "What a mega-hunk!"

"Mega-*what*?" Elizabeth asked in disbelief.

"That's what Robin and her friends call really cute guys," Jessica explained. "And Johnny definitely qualifies!"

"Johnny?" Elizabeth repeated.

"Johnny is Robin's *boyfriend*, Lizzie," Jessica said.

Elizabeth looked at her cousin in amazement. "But he looks so old," she began.

"He *is* older," Robin told her proudly. "Sixteen!"

Elizabeth's jaw dropped. Robin was a few months younger than her and Jessica. It was impossible to imagine her with a sixteen-year-old boyfriend.

"And that's not all," Jessica said. She lowered her voice to a whisper. "Johnny has his very own car. Can you believe it?" She looked at Robin with admiration and sighed. "I'm so jealous, Robin!"

Elizabeth didn't feel jealous. She felt amazed. "Does he have his license?" she asked.

"Of course he does." Robin laughed. "And guess what he drives?"

"What?" Jessica demanded.

"A red convertible!" Robin announced in a superior tone.

"That's so cool!" Jessica exclaimed.

"Can we meet him while we're here?" Elizabeth asked.

"Yeah, I can't wait!" Jessica put in. "When can we meet Johnny, Robin?"

"Meet him?" Robin repeated. She jumped off the bed and retrieved a hairbrush from the top of her dresser. "I'd love for you to meet Johnny," she said slowly as she ran the brush through her hair. "But he's visiting his grandparents in, um, Philadelphia."

"Oh, no!" Jessica said.

"But I haven't told you my *other* news," Robin added excitedly. "I've been asked to join the coolest, most exclusive club in our school. They're called the Jaguars. And only the most popular girls get to join!" For a moment, Robin's face darkened. "Actually, I'm not official yet. I still have to do my initiation. I'm a little nervous about that."

"Oh, don't worry about it," Jessica said confidently. "You'll be fine. And I should know, because I'm a member of the Unicorns, a club of the most popular girls at Sweet Valley Middle School!"

"You're kidding!" Robin said. "That sounds just like the Jags!"

"We call ourselves the Unicorns because unicorns are so special and beautiful. We have meetings every week, and our own table at lunchtime. And we all love the color purple, so we try to wear at least one purple thing every day."

"The Jaguars wear special silver I.D. bracelets. On one side your name is engraved. And on the back it says Jaguars." Robin smiled wistfully. "I can't wait to get one."

Elizabeth watched while Jessica and Robin returned to the yearbook. Robin was pointing out all the Jaguar members. *We'll talk about more interesting things soon*, she told herself. *I hope.*

All afternoon, Jessica and Robin talked about boys and clothes and their popular friends. For Elizabeth it was about as exciting as attending one of Jessica's Unicorn meetings. When Aunt Nancy called them for dinner, she was actually relieved.

While they ate, Uncle Kirk suggested that Jessica and Elizabeth might enjoy seeing the movies the family had taken during their year abroad.

"That sounds great!" Elizabeth exclaimed as she reached for the potatoes. "I'd love to hear about Paris." She turned to Robin. "Did you learn to speak French?"

"A little," Robin answered. "But we went to a school for Americans, so I only spoke it now and then."

"I can count to one thousand in French!" Stacey bragged.

"Please," Robin moaned. "Spare us!"

"Did you like the school?" Elizabeth asked Robin.

"Put it this way: I like it *much* better here!" Robin and Jessica exchanged knowing smiles, and Elizabeth knew Robin was thinking about Johnny and the Jaguars.

"Do we have to watch those boring movies?" Robin asked. "They'll just put Jessica and Elizabeth to sleep. And I've seen them a billion times!"

"It's up to your cousins," Aunt Nancy said. She passed a basket of blueberry muffins to Jessica. "Jessica, what would you like to do?"

"Well—" Jessica's eyes darted from Elizabeth to Robin. "I don't really care."

"Oh, gross," Robin remarked, rolling her eyes toward the ceiling.

"Robin," Aunt Nancy said, "Elizabeth and Jessica are interested in seeing where we lived and where you girls went to school."

"You'll even be able to see Robin's French boyfriend," Stacey teased.

"He wasn't my boyfriend, runt." Robin looked to Jessica for understanding. "He was just some guy who lived next door to us. I sort of thought he was OK-looking at the time."

"Jean-Luc was too your boyfriend!" Stacey argued.

"Now, Stacey, you know your father and I don't allow Robin to date yet," Aunt Nancy reminded her. "Jean-Luc was just a friend."

Elizabeth looked across the table at Jessica, but her sister was busy whispering to Robin. Elizabeth wondered if her aunt and uncle knew about Johnny. It certainly didn't sound like it.

Seven

◇

"Well, Jessica, now that you can say 'How much does that outfit cost?' in French, I guess you're ready to visit Paris," Uncle Kirk teased.

The movies had lasted most of the evening. In spite of Robin's protests, everyone enjoyed them—even Robin and Jessica. Aunt Nancy had made a huge bowl of popcorn, and Uncle Kirk had made funny comments while the tapes ran on the VCR.

"Dad, I have an idea," Robin said enthusiastically. "If we ever go back to France for a visit, can the twins come, too?"

"*Peut-être*," Uncle Kirk answered with a wink.

"What does that mean?" Jessica asked Robin as they headed back to her room.

"Maybe," Robin told her. "Your basic father-type answer."

When they got to Robin's room, the twins began unpacking. Each girl chose a cot, and they changed into their nightgowns.

"Doesn't this remind you of when we were little?" Elizabeth asked.

"Only better," Robin said. She sorted through the huge selection of makeup on top of her dresser. "I look at Stacey and I can't believe I was ever that age." Robin picked out a dark pink lipstick and began putting it on.

"Does Aunt Nancy let you wear that to school?" Jessica asked. She was obviously impressed.

"I can wear whatever I want," Robin answered.

"Can I try some?" Jessica asked eagerly. She joined Robin in front of the dresser and began examining her assortment of lipsticks.

Oh, no, Elizabeth thought. Jessica could spend hours trying to decide which lip gloss she preferred.

"Try this one." Robin handed Jessica a little pot of lip gloss. "This shade would be perfect with your complexion."

I wish I'd brought a book, Elizabeth thought. She watched as Jessica and Robin examined themselves in the round mirror over Robin's dresser.

I wish I'd brought Amy, too, Elizabeth added to herself.

"You know what I could really use right now?" Robin tossed her short hair and sighed dramatically.

"No, what?" Jessica asked.

"A cigarette," Robin said. "I'd give anything for one, but I'm all out."

"You smoke?" Elizabeth asked in astonishment. She couldn't believe it.

"Of course. I have for *ages*. All my friends do."

"Do your parents know?" Jessica asked casually. She reached for one of Robin's blush compacts and studied it with sudden interest.

"Give me a break!" Robin said. "Do either of you have a cigarette on you?"

Elizabeth opened her mouth to respond, but Jessica beat her to it.

"Normally, I would have some," she told Robin. "But I've had this terrible cold all week." Jessica made a little coughing noise and cleared her throat.

Elizabeth couldn't believe her ears. It was bad enough that Robin smoked. But to hear her own twin claim that *she* smoked, too, was more than

Elizabeth could take. She knew Jessica thought smoking was extremely dangerous.

"Robin, I can't believe you smoke!" Elizabeth said. "It's so bad for you!"

"Elizabeth, don't be such a baby!" Jessica exclaimed. She whirled around and gave her sister a superior look.

"Really, Elizabeth," Robin said.

"She's so immature," Jessica told Robin.

Elizabeth didn't know what to say. Without another word, she leaped from her cot and left the room. She ran straight to the bathroom and locked herself inside.

Don't be such a baby. The words went round and round in her head. Was she really so much more immature than everyone else?

Elizabeth sat down on the cold bathroom floor and began to cry. *If this is what growing up is like,* she thought miserably, *then you can keep it.*

Aunt Nancy made waffles the next morning in honor of Stacey's birthday. The twins' aunt and uncle had decorated the dining room with balloons and crepe paper. A big sign on the wall read HAPPY 8TH BIRTHDAY, STACEY!

"We have a special day planned for Stacey,

everybody!" Aunt Nancy announced when they had finished breakfast.

Stacey beamed. "On my birthday, you're not allowed to boss me around for the whole day, Robin," she said smugly.

Robin winked at the twins. "Whatever you say, Stace."

"Tell them where we're going, Mom!" Stacey said.

"We thought we'd spend the day at the zoo," Aunt Nancy said. "Stacey's inviting Maria and Kim."

"They're my two very best friends," Stacey explained to the twins.

"Oh, Mom, we don't really have to go, do we?" Robin asked, crossing her arms. "Jessica and Elizabeth went there the last time they came for a visit."

"I thought you'd enjoy it," Aunt Nancy said in surprise.

"Sure, if you like dying of boredom," Robin responded crossly.

"It *is* Stacey's birthday," Uncle Kirk reminded Robin. "And I doubt that a few hours at the San Diego Zoo will be fatal."

"I think it sounds like fun," Elizabeth said truthfully.

Robin and Jessica shared a look of disgust.

"Good. Then it's decided," Uncle Kirk said firmly. "Let's all be ready to go by ten, OK?"

"All right!" Stacey cried, dashing off to her bedroom.

Robin started to stand, but Aunt Nancy motioned her back into her seat. "There's something we wanted to discuss with you," she told Robin.

"What?" Robin asked.

"Your father and I decided you may have a slumber party tomorrow night—but on one condition."

"Mom, that's great!" Robin looked excitedly from Elizabeth to Jessica. "I didn't want to mention it to you until I was sure we could have it. But now we can plan it together! I want to invite all the Jaguars so you can meet them."

"Robin! How fantastic!" Jessica exclaimed.

"I love slumber parties!" Elizabeth added.

"What's the condition?" Robin asked her mother. "I promise we'll clean up afterwards."

"That's a relief." Aunt Nancy laughed. "But that's not what has your dad and me concerned."

"What then? I promise that no matter what you want, I'll do it!"

"We want you to invite Becky to the party," Uncle Kirk said.

"No!" Robin cried. "*Anything* but that!" She

turned to her mother. "Please, Mom," she said in a pleading voice, "don't make me invite her. *Please*."

"Becky is your friend," Aunt Nancy argued reasonably.

"Wrong," Robin said defiantly. "Becky *was* my friend."

"I seem to recall that before we went overseas, you and Becky were inseparable. And after we got back, up until a few weeks ago, you were best friends," Uncle Kirk said.

"That was before . . ." Robin hesitated.

"Before what?" Aunt Nancy inquired.

"Before I got asked to join the Jaguars," Robin muttered.

"Just because you have some new friends doesn't mean you should abandon the old ones," Aunt Nancy argued.

"Who's Becky, anyway?" Jessica asked.

"She's a hopeless goody-goody," Robin explained crossly. "A real nerd." She looked to Jessica for understanding. "We *used* to be friends. Kind of. But now we have absolutely nothing in common. *You* understand why I can't invite such a baby to my party," she concluded.

Jessica nodded. To her, it was obvious. "You know, I realize it's really none of my business . . ." Jessica began politely.

"Don't be silly, dear," Aunt Nancy said, smiling. "We'd like to hear what you have to say."

"Well, even if Robin did invite Becky, wouldn't it just be hard on her being around a bunch of girls who aren't her, um, type?"

Aunt Nancy frowned. "Jessica, I'm surprised at you! You sound just like Robin!"

"We're just trying not to hurt her feelings," Robin said defensively. She looked relieved to have Jessica on her side.

"Maybe if you gave her a chance to get to know the Jaguars, they'd invite Becky to join, too," Elizabeth suggested.

"Oh, sure, Elizabeth," Robin groaned. "And they'll probably invite *Stacey* while they're at it!"

"I think Elizabeth has a point," Uncle Kirk said. He reached for the last piece of bacon on the platter in the center of the table. "And besides, there's no point in trying to convince us, Robin. No Becky, no party."

Robin gave Jessica a pleading look. But Jessica just shrugged helplessly.

"Fine," Robin pouted. "I'll invite Becky. But she'll have a rotten time. And now, thanks to you, so will I!" She pushed back her chair and charged from the room. Elizabeth and Jessica followed Robin into the family room, where she sat hunched on the couch.

"Can you believe how unfair my parents are being?" she moaned.

"It's awful!" Jessica groaned sympathetically.

"It doesn't matter, Robin," Elizabeth said. "The important thing is that we get to have a slumber party and meet all your friends."

Robin managed to smile. "I suppose you're right, Elizabeth. You two are going to be so impressed by the Jaguars. And if that baby Becky has to come, so what?" She sat up, brightening. "I'm not going to let her ruin our fun!"

Elizabeth smiled uncomfortably. That wasn't exactly what she'd meant. Secretly, Elizabeth suspected she might have more in common with Becky than with the Jaguars—maybe because Robin had labeled Becky a baby. After all, last night Jessica and Robin had accused Elizabeth of the very same thing.

"Well, I might as well call Becky and get it over with," Robin said with a heavy sigh.

"Maybe she won't be home," Jessica suggested hopefully.

"Cross your fingers!" Robin laughed. She picked up the phone and began dialing. Halfway through the number, her eyes met Jessica's, and both girls began giggling.

"Jess!" Robin cried, slamming down the

receiver. "I'm never going to get through this call if you keep making me laugh!"

"I know!" Jessica's eyes lit up. "I'll go listen on the kitchen phone!"

"Great idea!" Robin said. "But be sure my parents are out of the kitchen."

"Coming, Elizabeth?" Jessica asked as she rose to go to the kitchen. "We can both listen in, as long as you promise not to giggle!"

"I don't think so, Jessica," Elizabeth said. She plopped down in a chair.

Robin waited for Jessica to run to the kitchen before dialing. When Becky answered the phone, Robin adopted her sweetest, most sincere voice.

"How can you be so mean?" Elizabeth demanded when Robin hung up the phone.

"Mean?" Robin asked, sounding genuinely surprised. "I invited her, didn't I?"

Jessica returned to the family room, shaking her head and laughing. "Oh, Elizabeth, don't give Robin a hard time," she exclaimed. "If you'd been listening, you'd know what a hopeless baby Becky is!"

Elizabeth gritted her teeth. "What is the matter with you two?" she demanded, jumping to her feet. "You never used to be this way!"

"What way?" Jessica asked in surprise.

"You know what way. You're acting snotty

and mean," Elizabeth said. "And I'm getting really tired of it!" She stormed out of the room.

"Wow, I've seen this on TV!" Stacey said excitedly, as she tore the wrapping paper off the twins' birthday gift. It was a board game called Detective.

"I used to love this game, Stacey," Elizabeth told her younger cousin. "It's like a mystery, and the winner is the first person to figure out 'whodunit'!"

"Can we all play after dinner?" Stacey asked.

"We'll see," Aunt Nancy answered, smiling.

"Great choice of presents, Lizzie!" Jessica teased her sister in a whisper. "*Now* look what you've gotten us into!"

"I guess you'd better come shopping with Mom and me next time, huh, Jess?" Elizabeth said.

The trip to the zoo earlier that day had been fun, although it seemed to Elizabeth that Jessica and Robin had tried their best not to have a good time. Still, Stacey and her two friends had a great time, and by the end, even Jessica and Robin seemed to be acting more like they used to.

After Stacey unwrapped the last of her presents, Robin suddenly jumped up from her chair.

"Oops," she said, "I almost forgot!" She rushed to her bedroom and retrieved a tiny box wrapped in pink tissue paper.

"Here, shrimp," she said when she returned, tossing the box to Stacey. "Happy birthday."

Stacey eagerly ripped off the wrapping. When she opened the box her mouth dropped open in amazement.

"Robin!" Stacey cried as she pulled out a tiny heart-shaped locket on a gold chain. In the center of the heart was Stacey's birthstone. "It's beautiful! You're the best sister in the whole world!" She ran over to give Robin a long hug.

"Yuck," Robin said with a tolerant sigh. "Stop drooling all over me, runt!" Everyone laughed. Stacey just hugged her sister tighter.

After dinner, Stacey convinced the family to play Detective. "It's my birthday till midnight," she reminded them. "That means I'm still the boss." It was nearly midnight when Stacey finally dozed off, and they put the game away.

As the twins and Robin got ready for bed, Elizabeth said, "You know, Robin, that locket you got Stacey was really beautiful."

Robin climbed into bed and shrugged. "Yeah," she said gruffly, "think of all the cigarettes I could have bought with the money I spent on it!" She rolled onto her side and cupped her chin in her palm. "You really think Stace liked it?" she asked Elizabeth softly.

"I think she loved it," Elizabeth reassured her. Elizabeth could tell from her cousin's smile that she was pleased.

Eight

◇

On Saturday afternoon, Elizabeth and Jessica lay on Robin's bed, watching as their cousin tried to decide what to wear to the slumber party. She pulled one outfit after another out of her closet, but nothing seemed to satisfy her.

"How about this one?" Robin asked in a muffled voice, her head half buried in her closet. She held out a dark blue blouse on a hanger.

"Too plain," Jessica pronounced.

"Elizabeth?" Robin asked. "What do you think?"

"I like it," Elizabeth answered distractedly. She was reading a book that she'd discovered buried under some magazines on Robin's desk.

Robin emerged from her closet and frowned at the twins. "You like everything I show you,

Elizabeth," she complained. "And you hate everything, Jessica. How am I supposed to decide what to wear tonight?"

"I told you what I thought. You should wear the black outfit you wore to the bus station Thursday," Jessica replied, sighing. She hated to admit it, but even *she* was getting a little bored with Robin's wardrobe dilemma. They'd already spent several hours preparing for the party. All morning they'd baked cookies and brownies and planned things to do. Robin had even insisted they clean up her room!

"Anyway, won't we all be wearing pajamas or nightgowns?" Elizabeth asked. "This *is* supposed to be a slumber party, after all."

"Besides, the Jaguars are your friends," Jessica added. "I know you want to impress them, but don't you think you're getting a little carried away?"

"You don't understand, either of you." Robin chewed nervously on her thumbnail. "If I don't do everything just right, the Jags might decide not to let me join."

Elizabeth set her book aside and cast a suspicious look at her cousin. "What exactly are their initiations like?"

"I don't know. Nothing I can't handle, I'm sure." Robin forced a smile. "My dad told me once about a fraternity at his college that made guys swallow a live goldfish for initiation! I hope it's nothing that gross!"

"Really!" Jessica shuddered. "Not even Steven would do that. And he'll eat anything!" She gave her cousin a reassuring smile. "I'm sure it will be a piece of cake, Robin."

Robin returned her attention to her closet. "As long as it's not a piece of fish!" she said, trying to laugh. She pulled out a denim miniskirt and held it up for the twins' inspection.

"Too casual," Jessica remarked.

"I like it," Elizabeth said.

"Oh, you two are no help at all!" Robin sighed loudly. She tossed the skirt onto the large pile of clothes accumulating on her floor. "Can you agree on *anything*?"

"No," said Jessica.

"Of course," Elizabeth answered at almost the same instant.

"See what I mean?" Robin groaned.

Elizabeth and Jessica exchanged a smile. "I think we can agree on one thing," Elizabeth said. "You're never going to decide what to wear at this rate, Robin. Why don't you go ahead and take a shower? While you're in the bathroom, Jessica and I will pick out something for you to wear."

Robin breathed a sigh of relief. "Thanks," she

said gratefully. She started to leave, then paused in the doorway. "Have I told you how glad I am that you're here? Especially now—I really need the moral support!" She smiled and disappeared down the hallway.

Jessica got up and began digging through the pile of discarded clothes in front of Robin's closet. "Personally, I still vote for the black outfit," she remarked. "You realize that no matter what we pick, Robin won't be satisfied." She turned her attention to the few clothes still remaining in Robin's closet. "What do you think she should wear, Elizabeth?"

"I don't care!" Elizabeth exclaimed. "You pick," she added more calmly. Then she lowered her voice to a whisper. "Don't you think Robin is awfully worried about having the Jaguars come over?"

Jessica abandoned her search of Robin's closet. "Now that you mention it, she does seem sort of worked up." She returned to Robin's bed and sat down on the edge. "Of course, I can't really blame her," she added. "Joining such a popular group of girls is a big deal for Robin. She's bound to be a little nervous. Wouldn't you be?"

"I don't know," Elizabeth answered thoughtfully. "I suppose so."

"Well, when I first joined the Unicorns, I

know *I* was nervous, too. Not as nervous as Robin," Jessica added, "but still, I can understand what she's going through."

"I have a feeling the Jaguars are different from the Unicorns, though."

"Different?" Jessica asked, sounding doubtful. "What do you mean, different?"

"There's all this initiation stuff, and the smoking . . ."

"They're just more mature, that's all," Jessica argued. She just didn't understand why Elizabeth couldn't accept the fact that Robin had changed. Jessica liked the "new" Robin, and she was sure she was going to like the Jaguars, too.

If this trip had proved anything, it was that Jessica was the mature one, after all. Elizabeth still had a lot of growing up to do—period or no period.

When the doorbell rang at eight that night, Robin sent the twins to answer it. She was still getting dressed.

Jessica swung the door open. Seven girls stood on the doorstep. They looked old, although she knew most of the Jaguars were the same age as the Unicorns. Most were wearing more makeup than her friends wore. All the girls had on the silver I.D. bracelets Robin had described. "You must be the Jags!" Jessica said brightly. "Come on in."

"Where's Robin?" a tall girl with black shoulder-length hair and pale blue eyes asked. She stepped into the hallway.

"She'll be down in a minute," Elizabeth said.

"Are you twins?" asked a second girl.

Elizabeth nodded. "I'm Elizabeth Wakefield, and this is my twin sister, Jessica. We're Robin's cousins."

"You aren't dressed alike," another Jaguar pointed out.

"Oh, we stopped doing that *ages* ago," Jessica assured her.

The rest of the Jaguars filed in, and the twins led them into the family room. Aunt Nancy and Uncle Kirk had promised Robin she could have the room to herself all night. They'd even vowed to keep Stacey out of Robin's hair until morning.

"So, which one of you is the president?" Jessica asked in a friendly tone. She glanced around the room. Several of the Jaguars had already settled onto the floor. One of them had turned on the TV and was playing with the remote control buttons.

"Me," the blue-eyed girl said. "I mean, I'm the leader. We don't exactly go in for elections."

For the first time since she'd arrived, she smiled at Jessica. "I'm Vicki Ellis. And this—" she motioned to a tall, pretty girl with curly blond hair who came over to join them, "is Lori Ann McCabe." Vicki chuckled loudly. "She's sort of our, uh, vice-president in charge of initiations."

"Hi, everybody!" Robin called as she entered the family room. She was wearing the black outfit Jessica had suggested, with all of her silver jewelry. Next to the Jaguars, who were all wearing jeans, her clothes seemed far too dressy.

"Hey, Robin," Vicki said, barely suppressing a smile. "You going to the prom or something?"

Jessica, who was dressed in her purple miniskirt and top, looked anxiously at her cousin. "We just got back from dinner," Jessica said quickly. "My aunt and uncle took us out to this really fancy place."

"Oh, *that* explains it," said Vicki with a wry smile.

"Did you two meet everybody?" Robin asked nervously.

"Just Vicki and Lori," Elizabeth told her.

"Well, that's Carla over there," Robin began. A petite girl with a haircut very much like Robin's waved her hand.

"And over there watching TV, that's Jackie, Shelby, Jeanne, and Renée."

"Hey, Robin," Jeanne said. "Where's the food?"

Robin's cheeks grew pink. "Oh, it's coming," she assured her. "We spent all day making brownies and cookies!"

"Robin's a regular little Betty Crocker!" Lori remarked with a smile.

"OK, well, you guys just get settled, and we'll go get the food—" Suddenly Robin paused, her eyes scanning the room. "Where are your sleeping bags?" she asked in a mystified voice. "Did you forget that this is a slumber party?"

Vicki rolled her eyes. "Slumber parties are for mega-dweebs," she informed Robin. "You didn't really think we were going to spend the whole night sitting in a circle and telling ghost stories, did you, Robin?"

Robin swallowed. "Well, of *course* not," she lied, as Elizabeth exchanged an anxious glance with Jessica.

"We only came because this is your big night, Robin!" Lori said, combing back a lock of hair with her fingertips.

"We've decided it's time for your initiation!" Vicki announced.

Just then the doorbell rang. Robin nearly jumped when she heard it.

"I'll get it," Elizabeth offered. She headed for the door and opened it.

"Hi," said the girl standing in the doorway. She was slightly plump, with an olive complexion and brown hair that hung in unruly waves. In her right hand she carried a pink sleeping bag, and in her left, a backpack.

"You must be Becky," Elizabeth said, returning the girl's shy smile.

"I hope I'm not late," Becky said as she stepped into the hallway. She examined Elizabeth's face more carefully. "I'll bet you're one of Robin's twin cousins," she said. "I almost feel like I know you; Robin's told me so many stories about you. The Three Musketeers, right?"

"Right!" Elizabeth laughed. "Here, let me help you with your stuff," she offered.

"Let me see," Becky said. "One of you is named Elizabeth, and the other is . . . Jennifer?"

"Jessica," Elizabeth corrected. "That's my sister."

"Nice to meet you, Elizabeth," Becky said. Suddenly she looked apprehensive. "Who else is here?" she asked.

"Just Robin, my sister, me, and all the Jaguars."

"Oh." Becky's face fell. "I was afraid of that."

She took a deep breath. "Well, come on," she said. "We might as well get this over with."

When Becky entered the family room, a hush fell over the group.

"Who invited *her*?" Vicki demanded.

"Why didn't you warn us, Robin?" Lori asked, giving Becky a scornful look.

Robin stood speechless. At last Elizabeth spoke up. "Do you know everyone, Becky?" she asked.

Becky nodded quietly. She set her sleeping bag and backpack down and approached Robin hesitantly. "Hi, Robin," she said. "Thanks for inviting me."

"Well, she may have invited you, but as far as *we're* concerned you're not coming on her initiation," Lori informed Becky.

"Initiation?" Becky repeated. "What initiation?"

"Robin's joining the Jaguars," Elizabeth explained.

"But you have to stay behind, *Rebecca*," Vicki said. "You and your sleeping bag. You are *definite* slumber party material."

Becky looked to Robin helplessly, but Robin wouldn't meet her eyes.

Elizabeth was shocked that her cousin

wouldn't say anything to defend Becky. How could she just ignore the way the Jaguars were treating her?

"What's my initiation going to be, Vicki?" Robin asked nervously, as though Becky didn't even exist. "Can you tell me yet?"

Vicki looked at Lori. Both girls grinned. "Well, all right," Vicki said at last. "I suppose we can tell you now."

The girls all settled on the floor, with Vicki in the center. Only Elizabeth and Becky hung back from the group.

"Your initiation," Vicki began in a low voice, "has to do with Johnny Anderson."

Elizabeth let out a sigh of relief. That didn't sound so bad. At least it involved Robin's boyfriend. How scary could it be? Strangely, though, Robin's face looked pale.

"Tonight, a little before midnight, you have to go to Johnny's house and sneak inside," Vicki continued. A couple of the Jaguars began to giggle, but Robin didn't look amused.

"Wake him up and get him to drive you to the park. We'll all be waiting there for you at midnight." Vicki grinned broadly. "Now, that's not so bad, is it, Robin?"

Robin swallowed hard and shook her head.

"You'll be a Jaguar in no time," Lori assured

her. "We're giving you an easy initiation because
we like you so much!"

Something was bothering Elizabeth. Robin
had said Johnny was visiting his grandparents in
Philadelphia. Robin couldn't perform her initiation
if Johnny wasn't home. From the look on Jessica's
face, Elizabeth could tell her twin was thinking
the same thing.

Elizabeth looked questioningly at Robin, ex-
pecting her to say something. But when Elizabeth
caught her cousin's eye, Robin just shook her
head and gave Elizabeth a warning glare.

"Robin," Elizabeth said, "why don't you and
Jessica and I go get the food?"

"Yeah, let's see some of those brownies,
Robin!" Shelby said.

"We'll be right back," Elizabeth told Becky.

Robin stood up and headed for the kitchen.
"I'll be back in a minute," she announced.

"Hurry up," Lori urged. "I'm starving!"

When they got to the kitchen, Robin began
taking the foil off a plate of chocolate-chip cookies.

"Robin, I thought Johnny was in Philadelphia," Elizabeth whispered. "Why didn't you say
anything to the Jaguars?"

"Um . . . he got back this afternoon. Didn't I
tell you?" Robin said. She looked at the floor as
she spoke.

"No," Elizabeth said shortly.

Robin shrugged. "We were just so busy this afternoon, I guess I forgot."

"At least now we'll get to meet him," Jessica said enthusiastically. "I can't wait."

"Yeah," Robin said uneasily. "Me either." She began arranging brownies on a plate. "So, what do you think of the Jags?"

"I think they're great!" Jessica said. She took a bite out of a cookie. "Really cool."

"Elizabeth?" Robin asked softly. "How about you?"

"Well, it's awfully soon to judge," Elizabeth said carefully. "Besides, what I think isn't important. It's what *you* think that matters, Robin."

Robin put her hand up to check her hair, then took a deep breath. "Well, I think the Jaguars are the most sophisticated, mature friends I've ever had. And I should feel honored that they want me to join." She almost sounded like she was trying to convince herself, Elizabeth thought.

"You're absolutely right," Jessica agreed as she reached for another cookie.

"I thought Vicki was awfully rude to Becky, though," Elizabeth said.

"Oh, please, Elizabeth!" Robin shot back. She was clearly annoyed. "Don't I have enough on my mind right now without worrying about *her*? I told my parents it was stupid to invite her." She shook her head angrily. "Becky's only been here five minutes and already she's embarrassed me!"

Without another word, Robin picked up the plate of brownies and stomped out of the room.

"Elizabeth, can't you see she's nervous? You really shouldn't nag her about Becky right now," Jessica warned.

"But why should Robin be nervous?" Elizabeth asked. "Her initiation doesn't sound very difficult."

"She's nervous because she wants to impress all her new friends," Jessica said. "You just don't understand."

Elizabeth watched her twin march out of the kitchen, carrying a platter of cookies. Nothing about this evening was making *any* sense to her. And it didn't get any better as the night wore on. Even Jessica noticed that Robin was getting more and more nervous. She decided a while later to take her cousin aside for a little pep talk.

"I think everybody's having a great time," Jessica whispered as she led Robin to one corner of the family room.

Robin gazed anxiously around the room. Most of the Jaguars were gathered in front of the TV, watching music videos. "Do you think we made enough food?" she asked. "Maybe we should have baked more cookies . . ." Her voice trailed off.

"*More* cookies?" Jessica echoed in amazement. They'd made enough for an army. Robin was taking this hostess thing too seriously. "If these were Steven's friends, I'd be worried about the cookie supply, but for the Jags, I think we made plenty," she reassured her cousin.

"Becky and Elizabeth sure are getting along well," Robin commented.

Jessica glanced toward the corner where Elizabeth and Becky had spent most of the evening talking to each other. Elizabeth certainly had a lot to learn about picking her friends! Jessica wouldn't be caught dead hanging around with someone like Becky. Just thinking about it was enough to make Jessica yawn. It was just more proof of Elizabeth's obvious immaturity.

At last, the clock on the fireplace mantel reached 11:30. Vicki and the other Jaguars gathered around Robin in a big circle. "Are you ready for your big moment?" Vicki asked Robin.

Robin nodded. Her face was very pale, and Jessica could have sworn her cousin was actually trembling.

"You go to Johnny's, and we'll all be waiting for you at the fountain in the park. You understand what you're supposed to do, don't you?"

"Of course she does," Jessica spoke up for her cousin.

"What if your parents notice that everyone's gone?" Elizabeth suddenly asked Robin.

"Becky can tell them we went on a scavenger hunt," Lori suggested in a nasty voice.

"I'm staying here with Becky," Elizabeth announced.

"Suit yourself," Vicki said indifferently.

Jessica looked at her twin and shook her head in disbelief.

As the group sneaked out the door, Elizabeth tapped Robin on the shoulder. "Be careful, OK?" she said.

Robin smiled nervously. "Thanks," she whispered.

Jessica was the last to leave. She looked back at Elizabeth and rolled her eyes. *What a baby*, she thought. Without a word, Jessica closed the door behind her as quietly as she could. She felt *very* mature.

Nine

"Why didn't you go with them?" Becky asked Elizabeth after the others were gone.

"I didn't want to," Elizabeth said flatly. She went to the picture window in the family room and peeked through the curtains. Jessica, Robin, and the Jags were nowhere in sight.

Elizabeth frowned. "Where does Johnny Anderson live, anyway?" she asked Becky.

"A few blocks from here, I think," Becky told her.

"And where is the park where the Jaguars are going?" Elizabeth asked.

Becky frowned. "Not too far. It's just on the other side of the neighborhood."

Elizabeth glanced nervously at the clock on the mantel. "I sure hope they get this over with quickly." She dropped down onto the couch. Becky joined her.

"You didn't have to stay here on my account, you know," Becky told Elizabeth.

"That's not why I stayed," Elizabeth explained. "I didn't want to have anything to do with Robin's stupid initiation."

"You mean you don't like the Hags?"

Elizabeth couldn't help but laugh. "The Hags?" she repeated.

"That's what I call the Jags. So do some of the other girls at school." Becky made a face. "I couldn't believe it when Robin started hanging around with them." She smiled ruefully. "Vicki really hates me. Did you notice?"

"It was kind of hard *not* to notice," Elizabeth said. She was relieved to see that Becky didn't seem to care about Vicki's rude behavior. In fact, Becky seemed to think it was almost funny. "Why doesn't she like you?"

"Because I wouldn't let her cheat off my paper during an important math test," Becky said with a sigh.

"I just can't figure out why Robin would want to be friends with them," Elizabeth said.

"Beats me." Becky shrugged. "I can't see why anyone would join the Hags. Maybe Robin likes their I.D. bracelets!" Suddenly she frowned. "You know, I've actually heard rumors at school about these Jaguar initiations."

"What kind of rumors?" Elizabeth asked with alarm.

Becky leaned close to Elizabeth. "Well, it's probably nothing, but there's a girl named Claire Smithers who went through a Hag initiation a few months ago."

"What happened to her?"

"No one knows for sure. But she stayed out of school for a whole week afterward. And when she came back she wouldn't tell anyone what had happened. She was probably just scared, or embarrassed, but still—"

"Becky, what if something happens?" Elizabeth asked nervously.

"Nothing's going to happen," Becky said. "They'll be back before you know it."

"We should have stopped Robin," Elizabeth said.

Becky shook her head. "I tried a couple of times. But once Robin got involved with the Jags, she didn't want to have anything to do with me."

"That must have really hurt your feelings," Elizabeth said sympathetically. She remembered how left out she'd felt when Jessica first joined the Unicorns.

"It did. To tell you the truth, I still don't

understand it. I guess Robin just wanted to belong to something. Being popular is very important to her."

That's how Jessica is, too, Elizabeth thought.

For a few moments the two girls sat silently. The ticking clock was the only noise in the house.

"You *do* think Robin and Jessica will be OK, don't you?" Elizabeth asked at last.

"I'm sure they'll be fine," Becky answered, but she didn't sound very convinced.

"Let's get one thing straight: you're coming with us to the park," Vicki told Jessica as they stood on the sidewalk a block away from Robin's house.

"Yeah, Robin's supposed to do her initiation by herself," Lori added firmly.

Jessica looked uncertainly at her cousin. Robin seemed very nervous, and it was awfully late for her to be out alone.

"Jessica's my guest, and I have to spend time with her," Robin told the Jags. "And she's only staying till tomorrow."

The Jaguars looked unconvinced, so Jessica spoke up. "I won't help her with the initiation. I'll just watch," she promised.

"Well, all right," Vicki said doubtfully. "I guess that would be OK."

"Remember, Robin, midnight in the park, *in* Johnny's car, if you want to be a Jaguar," Lori reminded her.

"I'll be there," Robin vowed.

"We'll be there," Jessica echoed, trying to sound confident. But as the Jags sauntered off down the street, she didn't *feel* very confident. It was very dark, with just a small sliver of moon up in the sky. Almost all of the houses on the street were in darkness.

"Now what?" Jessica asked.

"I don't know."

"Why don't we go to Johnny's house?" Jessica suggested reasonably.

"I . . . I guess we have to." Robin looked down and shook her head. "It's this way." She pointed down the street.

"This really is kind of exciting," Jessica said cheerfully as they began walking. Robin didn't answer her.

It was about two blocks to Johnny's, a big, two-story house surrounded by trees and thick bushes. Robin and Jessica stopped on the sidewalk across the street and looked at the house.

"I don't think I can go through with this," Robin whispered.

"Why not? Johnny's your boyfriend. I'm sure he'll understand and want to help out," Jessica said. "It's actually an easy initiation, when you think about it. Do the Jags know about you and Johnny?"

"Um, no."

"Lucky for you. They probably thought this would be the most embarrassing thing in the world. But since Johnny's your boyfriend it's really not so scary!"

"Um, it kind of *is* really scary, Jess," Robin mumbled. "I exaggerated a little bit."

"Exaggerated? About what?"

"Well, Johnny isn't exactly my boyfriend," Robin admitted.

"But you're really good friends, right?" Jessica asked hopefully.

"Not exactly."

"What do you mean 'not exactly'?" Jessica was beginning to get worried.

"He doesn't have any idea who I am," Robin confessed miserably.

"So you're supposed to sneak into the house of a boy you don't even know and get him to drive you to the park in the middle of the night?" Jessica exclaimed. "Are you absolutely sure you want to be a Jaguar?"

Robin looked uncertain for a moment. Then

she took a deep breath. "Yes, I want to be a Jag!" she said. "So I'm just going to have to do this."

"I'll wait right here." Jessica sat down on the curb.

"Oh, no you don't, Jessica! You're coming with me." Robin took her cousin's hand and pulled her to her feet. "What's the worst that can happen?"

Jessica didn't really want to know the answer to that question.

Slowly the girls crept across the lawn and climbed up the two stairs which led to the front door of the house.

"It's probably locked," Jessica said hopefully.

Robin reached out and turned the doorknob. "No such luck," she said.

She pushed the door open very gently, inch by inch. Slowly, the girls stepped inside—first Robin, then Jessica. Inside the front hall was a stairway.

"His room must be up there," Jessica whispered.

"He's going to think we're crazy!" Robin whispered back. "He'll probably call the police!"

"It's not too late to back out of this, you know."

"No." Robin shook her head forcefully. "I'm

going to do this. *Nothing* is going to make me leave here before I've asked Johnny. Nothing!"

They began making their way up the stairs. The second stair creaked loudly and both girls froze. Suddenly they heard a scratching noise.

Jessica grabbed Robin's arm. All at once, the scratching stopped. Jessica raised her head and forced herself to look up the stairs.

Staring back at her was a huge, tan-colored dog.

"Oh, no!" Robin hissed.

The dog let out a yelp and bounded down the stairs. Jessica and Robin turned around in panic.

"Run!" Jessica urged in a loud whisper, and both girls raced for the door. They didn't stop running until they were across the street. Looking back, they realized that the dog was nowhere in sight. But to their dismay, the front door was still wide open.

"We can't leave their door wide open like that!" Robin moaned.

"I'm *not* going back!" Jessica exploded. "We almost got caught! One more minute—" She stopped in mid-sentence. Something wet had just touched her hand. Slowly she looked down. The dog was licking her hand.

"Yuck!" Jessica cried.

"What's going on out here?" a male voice shouted.

"Great!" Robin moaned. "My life is now officially over!"

A flashlight beam blinded the girls. "What are you two doing out here?" the man's voice demanded.

"The, um . . . the dog was chasing us!" Jessica managed to say. It wasn't a very good answer, but she was too terrified to think up anything better.

"Oh," the man said. "Sorry. He must have gotten out. I guess I didn't close my front door all the way. Sorry if Bosco scared you."

Jessica couldn't believe they were going to get off this easy.

"Oh, that's all right, Mr. Anderson. He just surprised us," Robin said.

"Mr. Anderson?" the man echoed. "Why do you call me that?"

"Aren't you Johnny Anderson's father? Isn't this his house?" Robin asked.

"No. The Andersons are two doors down," the man said. "Well, good night. C'mon, Bosco!"

So far, Jessica thought, *this has definitely not been a good night*.

*   *   *

"How about a game?" Becky suggested to Elizabeth. "It will make the time go faster." Her eyes fell on the board game the Wakefields had given Stacey for her birthday. "We could play Detective."

Elizabeth shrugged. "All right, if you want." She peeked out the picture window one more time. "Becky, do you think I should wake my aunt and uncle and tell them about Robin?" Elizabeth asked anxiously.

Becky chewed on a fingernail. "I'm worried about Robin and Jessica, too," she finally said. "And I have to admit I thought about suggesting that you tell your aunt and uncle what's going on. But if you do, Robin and Jessica could get in so much trouble!"

"I know." It was a horrible choice to have to make. She'd never told on Jessica before—not in all the many times Jessica had gotten herself into tough scrapes. Jessica would never forgive her if she went to their aunt and uncle now. "But what if something goes wrong?" she asked. "I'd never forgive myself if something happened to Jessica and Robin!"

Becky pursed her lips. "How about if we give them a little more time? We'll play one game of Detective. Then we'll decide whether or not to wake your aunt and uncle."

"OK," Elizabeth agreed at last. "One game."

It was quarter past midnight when Becky finally won the game. As they started to put it away, Elizabeth heard a strange noise. "It's them!" she cried, leaping up.

But as she got to the hallway, it wasn't Jessica she found. It was Stacey.

"Stace!" she exclaimed. "What are you doing out of bed? It's so late!"

"I had to get a drink of water," Stacey said, rubbing her eyes. "Then I decided to sneak up on you and see the slumber party." She peered into the empty family room. "Where is everybody?" she asked. "Where are Robin and all her friends?"

"They'll be back any minute, Stace," Elizabeth told her. She knew that there was no point in lying to Stacey. She was too smart. And Elizabeth was a terrible liar.

"Back from where?" Stacey crossed her arms.

"Listen, do you know what time it is?" Elizabeth inquired, trying her best to sound like an angry parent.

"It's twelve-fifteen," Stacey answered smugly. She padded into the family room and stood directly in front of Becky. "Where's my sister and the rest of the slumber party?" she asked again.

"Why are you picking on me? Ask Elizabeth," Becky said.

Elizabeth sighed heavily. Things were getting more complicated by the minute. "Stacey, you're just going to have to trust me," she said at last. "Robin will be home very soon. And there's no reason to worry."

"Really?" Stacey examined Elizabeth's face closely, as though she didn't quite believe her cousin. "Promise?"

"Of course I promise. Now you better get back to bed before your mom and dad hear you. Midnight is a little past your bedtime, after all."

"It's past *your* bedtime, too," Stacey pointed out. She looked from Becky to Elizabeth one last time. Then she turned on her heels and headed down the hallway.

"Good night, Stacey," Elizabeth called.

"Whew." Becky heaved a sigh of relief. "That was a close one!"

"Yes, but I still don't know what to do," Elizabeth said nervously.

"It *is* awfully late," Becky agreed. "It didn't sound so bad when they were all talking about being out past midnight. But now it's kind of creepy. I know *I* wouldn't want to be out this late! And my folks would kill me!"

"So would mine," Elizabeth agreed.

"What do you think your aunt and uncle will do to Robin if we wake them up and tell them?"

"I don't know exactly, but I bet they won't be happy."

"*That's* the understatement of the century!" Becky laughed.

Elizabeth shook her head. "Whenever Jessica's been in a jam before, I've always been able to help her out. But this time . . . well, I need some help!"

Becky suddenly cleared her throat loudly. "A-hem."

"But I've never, ever told on Jessica before," Elizabeth continued. "What if she's fine? She'll be mad at me for a week!"

Becky cleared her throat again, more loudly this time. "*A-hem!*"

"But maybe that doesn't matter," Elizabeth went on. "Even if Jessica is mad at me forever, I'll have to tell Aunt Nancy and Uncle Kirk."

"You're right about *that*," Becky said.

Elizabeth looked up and noticed that Becky's face was pale. "What do you mean?"

Silently, Becky pointed a finger toward the hallway.

Even before she spun around, Elizabeth had a feeling she knew what she would find.

There, standing in the hallway, was Stacey. Right behind her were Elizabeth's aunt and uncle. And as Elizabeth had predicted, they were definitely not happy.

Ten

Elizabeth, Becky, and Stacey stood by the family room window, peeking through the curtain.

"What do you think my mom and dad will do to Robin, Elizabeth?" Stacey asked.

Elizabeth shook her head. "I don't know, Stace." The truth was, she was afraid to even *think* about what her aunt and uncle might do. When they had left to find the girls, they'd looked as angry as Elizabeth had ever seen anyone look.

"Do you think they'll ground her?" Stacey wondered.

"Maybe," Elizabeth admitted.

"I bet they ground her until she graduates from high school," Stacey said unhappily. "And it will be my fault."

"No, it won't, Stacey," Becky reassured her.

"If Robin gets into any trouble it will be her own fault, not yours."

"I shouldn't have told!" Stacey exclaimed. "But I was so worried when I saw that everyone was gone."

Elizabeth put her arm around Stacey's shoulder. "You did the right thing, Stacey. We were just about to wake up your mom and dad anyway."

"It's them!" Becky cried suddenly as Uncle Kirk pulled into the driveway.

"Stacey, I promised your mom you'd be in bed by the time they got back!" Elizabeth said urgently. "Quick, run to bed and at least pretend to be asleep, OK? Now that you see Robin's home safe and sound, you can relax."

"But it's just getting interesting!" Stacey protested.

"Hurry, Stacey!" Elizabeth urged.

"Oh, all right." Stacey trudged toward the hallway. "But tell Robin I'm really sorry."

"Don't worry," Elizabeth reassured her. "She'll understand." Secretly, she wasn't so sure either Jessica or Robin would be in a very forgiving mood.

She peered outside at the station wagon. Aunt Nancy, Jessica, and Robin were just getting out. All the Jaguars remained in the car.

"I suppose your uncle is going to drive all the Hags home," Becky said. "How humiliating for them."

"I guess if they'd brought their sleeping bags, they could have spent the night," Elizabeth said.

"Did you see your aunt's expression?" Becky whispered.

"Bad?"

"It reminds me of the way my mom looked when she found out my brother tried to drive her car and knocked a hole in the garage door."

Elizabeth frowned. She was even more concerned about the look of rage she saw on Jessica's face. Robin didn't look too pleased, either.

As the front door opened, Becky whispered, "I'm going to the bathroom. Call me when it's all over."

"No way!" Elizabeth grabbed Becky's arm. "I may need you for protection!"

Just then Aunt Nancy stepped into the hallway, followed by Jessica and Robin. "We'll talk about this tomorrow, Robin," she said quietly.

"But, Mom—" Robin objected.

"Tomorrow," Aunt Nancy said firmly. "Now get some sleep, all of you."

Jessica and Robin came into the family room. For a few seconds, no one spoke.

"Are you two all right?" Elizabeth finally asked.

" Do you really care?" Jessica snapped angrily.

"Of course we care!" Elizabeth exclaimed. "We've been worried sick about you!"

"So you told Uncle Kirk and Aunt Nancy where we were? Thanks, Elizabeth," Jessica said. "Thanks a whole lot."

"What happened with the initiation, anyway?" Becky asked softly.

Robin opened her mouth to answer, but Jessica beat her to it. "It was going great," she said, giving Elizabeth a cold stare. "Until you two ruined everything."

"Jess, I'm sorry!" Elizabeth said, her voice wobbly. "But I was so afraid something might have happened to you . . ."

"What makes you think *you're* so mature that you have to take care of me?" Jessica demanded.

"What does maturity have to do with it?" Becky interrupted. "Elizabeth was just trying to be a good sister."

"I don't *need* a baby-sitter, thank you," Jessica said. Her cheeks were deep red and her lower lip was trembling. "And as far as I'm concerned, I don't need a sister, either!" She ran down the hallway toward Robin's bedroom. Elizabeth watched in disbelief.

Robin followed Jessica. "I wish this night had never happened," she muttered under her breath.

"Me, too," Elizabeth whispered.

That night, Jessica and Robin slept in Robin's room, and Elizabeth and Becky slept in the family room. When they woke up the next morning, Becky told Elizabeth she didn't think it would be a good idea for her to stay for breakfast. "I think I should let Robin cool off a little," Becky explained as she rolled up her sleeping bag.

"Just promise me you'll call Robin in a day or two, OK?" Elizabeth said. "Maybe you two can be friends again, once she's had a chance to think things over."

"I will," Becky promised.

After Becky called her father to ask him to pick her up, the two girls walked outside to the front yard to wait.

"What about you and Jessica?" Becky asked. "Do you think she's ready to forgive you?"

Elizabeth tried to smile. "I'm not so sure about that," she said truthfully.

"Well, she'll have to make up with you eventually, right? After all, you *are* sisters. How long can you share the same bathroom with someone without talking to her?"

"I think I'm going to find out," Elizabeth said glumly.

Becky waved to her father when he pulled into the driveway. "I'm glad I met you, Elizabeth," she said with a grin. "It may not have been a typical slumber party, but it sure was interesting!"

"I'm glad I met you, too," Elizabeth told her.

Becky jumped into the front seat and closed the door. "Have a good trip home!"

Elizabeth watched as Becky and her father drove out of view. She was almost afraid to go inside and face Jessica and Robin, but she knew she couldn't avoid them forever.

She found them in the kitchen with Stacey. They were all eating bowls of cereal. When no one else spoke, Elizabeth asked, "Where's Aunt Nancy and Uncle Kirk?"

"They're getting dressed," Stacey answered. She was still wearing her flannel pajamas and her hair was crumpled from sleep.

"Is Becky gone?" Robin asked quietly.

"She just left." Elizabeth walked over to the cupboard and began making herself a bowl of cereal.

"Good," Jessica muttered. "That means there's only one traitor left."

"Just because I was worried about you does not mean I'm a traitor!" Elizabeth cried.

"*I'm* the traitor! You should be yelling at me," Stacey interrupted.

"What do you mean, Stace?" Robin asked, narrowing her eyes.

"*I'm* the one who woke up Mom and Dad," Stacey admitted. "It was so late, and you were all gone. When Elizabeth and Becky wouldn't tell me where you were, I got worried."

Elizabeth cast a reassuring glance at Stacey. "Stace, I told you last night that Becky and I were just about to wake up your Mom and Dad. We were just as worried as you were." She hated to give Jessica even more reason to be angry with her, but Elizabeth couldn't stand to see Stacey feel so guilty.

"Besides, Elizabeth is the one who told your Mom and Dad where we were, Stacey," Jessica pointed out, giving Elizabeth a cold stare.

Stacey gazed at Robin sadly. "Still, if Mom and Dad punish you, it'll be partly my fault, Robin. I'm sorry, really I am." She hung her head, adding softly, "I guess you'll want me to give you back my necklace now."

Robin shook her head and sighed. "Come here, squirt," she said quietly.

Stacey stood next to her sister at the table,

and Robin gave her an affectionate hug. "Of course I'm not going to take your necklace back. What gave you an idea like that?"

"Well, I saw how mad you and Jessica were at Elizabeth . . ." Stacey began.

"That's different," Jessica interrupted. She stared into her cereal bowl, refusing to meet Elizabeth's eyes. "Elizabeth's more"—she paused—"*mature.*"

"Jessica!" Elizabeth cried angrily. But she could tell her sister was in no mood to be reasoned with.

"I'm sorry you and Jessica are going to be in trouble," Stacey said.

"Oh, what's the worst that could happen?" Robin asked. "So they ground me for a week. That's not the end of the world!"

"How does a month grab you?" Uncle Kirk said sternly as he came into the kitchen, followed by Aunt Nancy.

"A month?" Robin cried. "But Dad, that's so unfair!"

"And that's not all," Aunt Nancy added. "Your father and I are going to call the parents of all the girls who went to the park last night and tell them what happened." She gave Jessica a meaningful look. "And I mean *all* the parents. I think your mother and father are going to be very disappointed in you, Jessica."

"I'm really sorry, Aunt Nancy," Jessica said sincerely. "I guess we just weren't thinking."

"*I'll* say you weren't," Uncle Kirk said. He walked over to the counter and began making coffee. "Did you think for a minute about how dangerous the park could be at that hour?"

"No," Jessica mumbled, hanging her head.

"And did you think about how worried we would be about your safety?" Aunt Nancy demanded.

"You weren't supposed to wake up," Jessica explained.

"That's *hardly* the point, Jessica." Aunt Nancy shook her head. "If you girls want to be treated like adults, you have to act like adults. And that means behaving responsibly and not taking stupid risks. The world isn't always a safe place, I'm afraid."

"And if your friends try to pressure you, we expect you to be strong enough and smart enough to make your own decisions," Uncle Kirk said.

"What happened when you took the Jaguars home last night?" Robin asked meekly.

Uncle Kirk smiled for the first time that morning. "Well, I made sure each girl made it safely nside her house. They were awfully quiet during the ride, I must say."

"I'm really sorry I messed up so bad, Mom and Dad," she said apologetically. "I guess I just wanted to be a Jaguar so much that I sort of lost track of everybody else."

"Like Becky," Aunt Nancy pointed out as she pulled two coffee mugs from the cupboard.

"Yeah, Becky," Robin said sadly. "Maybe after we take you guys to the bus station today, I'll ride my bike over to her house and try to apologize."

"I think that's a fine idea," Uncle Kirk remarked.

"Great," Robin said with a relieved grin.

"Unfortunately, you're grounded."

Robin's face fell. "I was afraid you'd remember that."

"Good try, Robin," Stacey whispered.

"Now, how about some *real* breakfast? Something more than just cereal?" Aunt Nancy asked cheerfully. "We can't let the twins go home with empty stomachs!"

"Thanks, Aunt Nancy, but I'm not very hungry," Elizabeth said softly.

"Me either," Jessica said. "May I be excused so I can start packing?"

"Of course," Uncle Kirk said exchanging a

worried glance with his wife. "Your bus leaves in an hour and a half."

It's going to be a long ride home, Elizabeth thought glumly as she followed Jessica out of the kitchen.

Eleven

◇

Jessica gave the driver her ticket and walked down the aisle of the bus. Reluctantly, she sat down next to her twin. Elizabeth was peering out the window and waving. "Stacey won't stop waving goodbye," she explained.

Elizabeth leaned back in her chair as the bus pulled away from the station. "She's so cute," she remarked.

When Jessica didn't say anything, Elizabeth added, "Stacey, I mean. Sometimes I wonder what it would be like to have a little sister."

"Why? So you can ruin her life, too?" Jessica snarled.

"Jessica, are you going to stay mad at me *forever*?" Elizabeth asked desperately.

"Yes!" Jessica shifted in her seat so that she

was facing away from her sister. "How can I ever trust you again? One of us has really changed, Elizabeth. And it's not me!"

"Jess, *you're* the one who's changed!" Elizabeth shot back. "And, just for your information, I'm awfully tired of hearing about last night. I was only trying to help you, and you know it."

"There's no point in discussing it, Elizabeth. I'm not going to be talking to you anymore."

"For how long?" Elizabeth asked quietly.

"Forever." Jessica curled up in her seat, closed her eyes, and tried to pretend that Elizabeth didn't exist. Somehow, Jessica was managing to feel guilty and mad and depressed all at the same time. And as if that weren't enough, she had a stomach ache, too.

Cheer up, she told herself. *Maybe when I wake up, I'll feel better.*

"Wake up, Jess!" Elizabeth exclaimed.

Jessica awoke from a deep sleep to find all the passengers getting off the bus. She didn't even remember falling asleep.

"What's going on?" she demanded groggily, forgetting that she wasn't speaking to Elizabeth. "We're not there yet, are we?"

"We're about halfway there," Elizabeth told

her. "We have to change to a different bus in this town, remember? Uncle Kirk explained it to us on the way to the bus station."

"Oh, yeah," Jessica mumbled as she stood up. Actually, she didn't remember. She'd been too busy giving Elizabeth the silent treatment on the way to the station, to pay much attention to the conversation.

The twins climbed off the bus with the other passengers. The bus had parked in front of a small, red brick station. The driver pointed out the empty bus that would take them the rest of the way to Sweet Valley.

There was more room on the new bus, and Jessica managed to get her own seat two rows away from Elizabeth. *There*, she thought as she sat down out of view of her twin, *that'll show her*.

Jessica waited impatiently for the bus driver to arrive. But after several minutes, no one had appeared.

Jessica's stomach still ached a little, and she thought that some ginger ale might make her feel better. She peered out the window at the bus station. There was probably a soda machine inside, and it would only take her a minute to run in and get something to drink. Besides, they wouldn't exactly drive off and leave her behind, would they? Elizabeth would make the driver wait.

Jessica reached for her purse and stood up. She was halfway down the aisle when she heard Elizabeth's voice. "Jess!" Elizabeth called to her. "Where are you going? The bus will be leaving any minute!"

Jessica kept right on going. Since she and Elizabeth were officially no longer speaking, there was no need to answer her.

Inside the little bus station, Jessica found a vending machine. She bought a ginger ale and glanced out the door at her bus. There was still no sign of a driver, so she decided to look around the station.

Jessica took a sip of her ginger ale. Unfortunately, it didn't seem to help her stomach, at all. This was probably a different kind of stomach ache—like one caused by worrying about what her parents were going to say when she got home. Now that they were halfway to Sweet Valley, she was starting to worry about what awaited her when she got there. It was pretty safe to assume that Aunt Nancy and Uncle Kirk would tell the Wakefields they'd grounded Robin for a whole month.

Jessica finished her ginger ale and headed back to the parking lot. *A whole month*, she thought grimly. Four entire weeks without Unicorn meetings, or Boosters practice, or trips to the mall—

"No!" Jessica cried out suddenly as she glanced toward the bus. "Wait!" The bus was pulling away! It was impossible for Jessica to catch up to it. As the bus turned a corner out of the station, Jessica strained for a glimpse of Elizabeth. How could her own sister abandon her this way? Jessica realized that she was all alone—and she didn't even know where she was! "Now what am I going to do?" Jessica moaned as hot tears filled her eyes.

"Good question!"

Jessica whirled around to see her twin standing behind her.

"Lizzie! I was afraid you'd left me!" Jessica gave her sister a long hug, as tears of relief spilled down her cheeks.

"I got worried when you were gone so long," Elizabeth explained. She sounded annoyed. "We're stuck here until the next bus to Sweet Valley shows up."

"When will that be?" Jessica wiped away a tear.

"Uncle Kirk told me there would be another bus to Sweet Valley a couple of hours after ours," Elizabeth told her. "In the meantime, *you* can call Mom and Dad and explain why we're late."

"Couldn't you call them, Lizzie?" Jessica pleaded. "I'm in enough trouble as it is."

Elizabeth rolled her eyes. "It's not *my* fault we're stranded here."

"I know," Jessica said softly.

"And it's not *my* fault you got into trouble."

"I know."

"Well then, why are you so mad at me!" Elizabeth exploded.

Jessica tried to come up with a good answer, but all she could think of was how glad she was to know Elizabeth wasn't on the bus to Sweet Valley without her. "You want to know the truth, Lizzie?" she said at last. "I'm *glad* you worried about me this time. I don't know what I would have done if I'd been left behind by myself."

The girls began walking back to the station. "And you know what else?" Jessica added.

"No, what?"

Jessica took a deep breath. "I'm even glad you were worried about me last night." She chuckled under her breath. "The truth is, *I* was worried about me, too!"

The twins sat down on a bench in a corner of the station. "What happened last night, Jessica?" Elizabeth asked. "That is, if you want to talk about it."

"You won't believe it," Jessica moaned. "It

was the most humiliating night of my whole life! As soon as we sneaked out the door, Robin confessed to me that Johnny wasn't really her boyfriend! In fact he doesn't even know who she is! She just made up that whole story to impress us."

"Really! That explains why she didn't want us to meet him!"

"Anyway, when we got outside, she begged me to go to his house with her to help with her initiation. Of course I said yes. I felt so sorry for Robin. She wanted to join the Jags so badly, and I thought maybe I could help."

"What happened when you got to the house?"

Jessica sighed. "We sneaked inside and got halfway up the stairs before this monstrous, slobbering dog chased us out the door."

"You're kidding!"

"Then this man came outside and started yelling at us—"

"Johnny's father?" Elizabeth prompted.

"Not exactly."

"Who was it, then?"

"We didn't stick around for introductions," Jessica smiled wryly. "But he *definitely* wasn't Johnny's dad. We were at the wrong house!"

Elizabeth's eyes grew wide. "What did you do then?"

"By that time even Robin was ready to give

up. We went back to the park and told the Jaguars what had happened. Vicki said she'd give Robin another chance at an initiation."

"I'll bet Robin was relieved," Elizabeth said.

Jessica nodded grimly. "Yeah, until she heard what the Jags wanted her to do."

"Was it hard?"

"No. It was *mean*. Vicki wanted Robin to go back home and wait until Becky fell asleep. Then she was supposed to take a pair of scissors and cut off Becky's hair!"

"That's horrible!" Elizabeth cried.

"I know. Robin told the Jags she didn't want to have anything to do with people who could be that cruel. I was really proud of the way she told them off." Jessica shook her head. "They're not anything like the Unicorns, you know. I'm glad Robin didn't join their group."

"Me, too," Elizabeth agreed. Suddenly her eyes clouded. "But why didn't you two tell Becky and me what happened when you got home?"

Jessica shrugged. "I guess we were both too embarrassed about the whole night to want to talk about it. It didn't exactly turn out like we'd planned. But I don't mind telling you that Robin and I were awfully glad to see Uncle Kirk and Aunt Nancy drive up!" Jessica gave her twin a smile. "And they wouldn't have been there, if it weren't for you and Becky and Stacey. You did the right thing."

"Well, I'm just glad everything turned out OK," Elizabeth told her.

Jessica looked at the floor. "I've been such a jerk to you lately, Lizzie," she said softly. "I'm really sorry."

"That's OK," Elizabeth said with a smile. "After all, we've both been going through a lot of changes lately."

Jessica took a deep breath. "There's something else I wanted to tell you, Lizzie. You know when we got our periods?"

"Yes. What about it?"

"Well, *we* didn't get our periods. *You* did."

Elizabeth looked thoroughly confused. "What are you talking about, Jessica? Of course we got our periods!"

Jessica shook her head. "No. I only pretended to, because I was too ashamed to admit the truth. And all week I've been trying to make up for it by acting more mature than you. I guess I didn't do a very good job." She paused, waiting to hear Elizabeth's angry response.

But Elizabeth just put her arm around Jessica and gave her a squeeze. "Oh, Jess. Everybody's different. You'll start when you're ready."

"I suppose." Jessica tried to smile. "It just

doesn't seem fair, though. You got to be born first, too!"

"I was only four minutes ahead, you know," Elizabeth reminded her.

Jessica stood up and stretched. "I'm going to get another soda," she said. "Want one?"

"No, thanks." Elizabeth stood up, too, and glanced around the station. "There's a pay phone over there. I'll go call Mom and Dad."

"Thanks, Lizzie," Jessica said gratefully. "You're the greatest."

On her way to the vending machine, Jessica decided to go to the ladies' room. As she pushed open the bathroom door, she glanced over her shoulder and caught sight of Elizabeth putting a coin into the telephone. *Thank goodness Lizzie's calling Mom and Dad*, she thought with relief. *I wonder how long they'll ground me for.*

After the door was closed, she entered a stall. *Maybe I can get out of it if I offer to do all the chores, even Steven's and Elizabeth's.*

Suddenly Jessica gasped out loud. "I can't believe it!" she cried. Jessica had started her period! *So I guess I've caught up with Elizabeth, after all*, Jessica thought with relief.

Elizabeth was just hanging up the phone when Jessica came rushing into the station lobby. "Everything's all set," Elizabeth said. "Dad will pick us up when we get into Sweet Valley." She examined Jessica more closely. "Jess, are you OK?"

Jessica couldn't help grinning. "I've never been better. Do I look any different to you?"

"Different?" Elizabeth repeated uncertainly. "How?"

"Oh, I don't know," Jessica said slyly. "More mature, maybe?"

Elizabeth returned Jessica's smile. "You don't mean . . ."

Jessica nodded excitedly. "Just now!"

"Jess, that's great! Congratulations!" Elizabeth cried. "So what do you have to say, now that you're so much more mature?"

Jessica thought for a moment. This was, after all, a big moment in her life. She should say something serious.

"Fabulous!" she exclaimed.

"Do you think things will change now that we're *women*?" Elizabeth asked Jessica once they were safely on the bus headed for Sweet Valley.

"I think *I'll* be a lot less popular," Jessica replied. "Especially since I'm going to be grounded forever."

Elizabeth giggled. "Maybe if you explain to Mom and Dad, they'll be easy on you."

"I hope so!" Jessica exclaimed. "If they're really mad, I might not be able to go to my high school prom."

"Or to your sweet sixteen party," Elizabeth put in.

"And when boys ask me out on dates," Jessica said, "I'll have to say I'm *still* grounded."

"Jess!" Elizabeth exclaimed. "You're so boy crazy, you sound almost like a teenager!"

"Oh well," Jessica said lightly. "It won't be long before you like boys, too. And not just as friends."

"That'll be the day," Elizabeth replied. But secretly, she wasn't so sure her sister was wrong.

Will Elizabeth become as boy crazy as Jessica? Find out in Sweet Valley Twins 43, **Elizabeth's First Kiss.**

We hope you enjoyed reading this book. If you would like to receive further information about available titles in the Bantam series, just write to the address below, with your name and address: Kim Prior, Bantam Books, 61–63 Uxbridge Road, Ealing, London W5 5SA.

If you live in Australia or New Zealand and would like more information about the series, please write to:

Sally Porter
Transworld Publishers
(Australia) Pty Ltd
15–23 Helles Avenue
Moorebank
NSW 2170
AUSTRALIA

Kiri Martin
Transworld Publishers (NZ) Ltd
Cnr. Moselle and Waipareira
Avenues
Henderson
Auckland
NEW ZEALAND

All Bantam and Young Adult books are available at your bookshop or newsagent, or can be ordered at the following address: Corgi/Bantam Books, Cash Sales Department, PO Box 11, Falmouth, Cornwall, TR10 9EN.

Please list the title(s) you would like, and send together with a cheque or postal order. You should allow for the cost of book(s) plus postage and packing charges as follows:
80p for one book
£1.00 for two books
£1.20 for three books
£1.40 for four books
Five or more books free.

Please note that payment must be made in pounds sterling; other currencies are unacceptable.

(The above applies to readers in the UK and Republic of Ireland only)

BFPO customers, please allow for the cost of the book(s) plus the following for postage and packing: 80p for the first book, and 20p for each additional copy.

Overseas customers, please allow £1.50 for postage and packing for the first book, £1.00 for the second book, and 30p for each subsequent title ordered.

Jessica and Elizabeth Wakefield have had lots of adventures in *Sweet Valley High* and *Sweet Valley Twins* . . .

Now read about the twins at age seven! You'll love all the fun that comes with being seven – birthday parties, playing at dressing-up, class projects, putting on puppet shows and plays, losing a tooth, caring for animals and much more! It's all part of *Sweet Valley Kids*. Read them all!

THE SADDLE CLUB

An exciting series by Bonnie Bryant, available wherever Bantam paperbacks are sold.

Share the thrills and spills of three girls drawn together by their special love of horses in this adventurous series.

First Kiss

First love . . . first kiss!

A terrific series that focuses firmly on that most important moment in any girl's life – falling in love for the very first time ever.

Available from wherever Bantam paperbacks are sold!

1. HEAD OVER HEELS by Susan Blake
2. LOVE SONG by Suzanne Weyn
3. FALLING FOR YOU by Carla Bracale
4. THE PERFECT COUPLE by Helen Santori